"Mac

The genuine concern in Eve's voice brought a lump of emotion to his throat, making it impossible for him to respond. He leaned forward to rest his elbows on his knees, keeping his gaze averted from hers.

Her hand came out to cover his in a gesture that stole his breath and brought his heart to a shuddering halt before it raced off once more.

Mac couldn't recall the last time anyone had touched him simply to offer comfort. Beneath her fingers he could feel her warmth seeping into him, spreading through him like a healing balm, awakening an emotion he didn't want to feel.

He'd grown accustomed to spending time alone, telling himself he liked it that way, that he preferred peace, quiet...distance.

But he'd never met a woman like Eve.

Dear Reader,

Grab a front-row seat on the roller-coaster ride of falling in love. This month, Silhouette Romance offers heart-spinning thrills, including the latest must-read from THE COLTONS saga, a new enchanting SOULMATES title and even a sexy Santa!

Become a fan—if you aren't hooked already!—of THE COLTONS with the newest addition to the legendary family saga, Teresa Southwick's *Sky Full of Promise* (#1624), about a stone-hearted doctor in search of a temporary fiancée. And single men don't stay so for long in Jodi O'Donnell's BRIDGEWATER BACHELORS series. The next rugged Texan loses his solo status in *His Best Friend's Bride* (#1625).

Love is magical, and it's especially true in our wonderful SOULMATES series, which brings couples together in extraordinary ways. In DeAnna Talcott's *Her Last Chance* (#1628), virgin heiress Mallory Chevalle travels thousands of miles in search of a mythical horse—and finds her destiny in the arms of a stubborn, but irresistible rancher. And a case of amnesia reunites past lovers—but the heroine's painful secret could destroy her second chance at happiness, in Valerie Parv's *The Baron & the Bodyguard*, the latest exciting installment in THE CARRAMER LEGACY.

To get into the holiday spirit, enjoy Janet Tronstad's *Stranded with Santa* (#1626), a fun-loving romp about a rodeo megastar who gets stormbound with a beautiful young widow. Then, discover how to melt a Scrooge's heart in Moyra Tarling's *Christmas Due Date* (#1629)

I hope you enjoy these stories, and please keep in touch!

Mary-Theresa Hussey

Mary-Theresa Hussey
Senior Editor

Please address questions and book requests to:
Silhouette Reader Service
U.S.: 3010 Walden Ave., P.O. Box 1325, Buffalo, NY 14269
Canadian: P.O. Box 609, Fort Erie, Ont. L2A 5X3

Christmas
Due Date

MOYRA TARLING

SILHOUETTE *Romance*®

Published by Silhouette Books

America's Publisher of Contemporary Romance

To Judy and Bonnie, two great friends! Thanks.

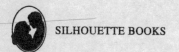 SILHOUETTE BOOKS

ISBN 0-373-19629-6

CHRISTMAS DUE DATE

Copyright © 2002 by Moyra Tarling

This edition published by arrangement with Harlequin Books S.A.

Visit Silhouette at www.eHarlequin.com

Printed in U.S.A.

Books by Moyra Tarling

Silhouette Romance

MOYRA TARLING

was born and raised in Aberdeenshire, Scotland. It was there that she was first introduced to and became hooked on romance novels. In 1968, she immigrated to Vancouver, Canada, where she met and married her husband. They have two grown children. Empty-nesters now, they enjoy taking trips in their getaway van and browsing in antique shops for corkscrews and button-hooks. But Moyra's favorite pastime is curling up with a great book—a romance, of course! Moyra loves to hear from readers. You can write to her at P.O. Box 161, Blaine, WA 98231-0161.

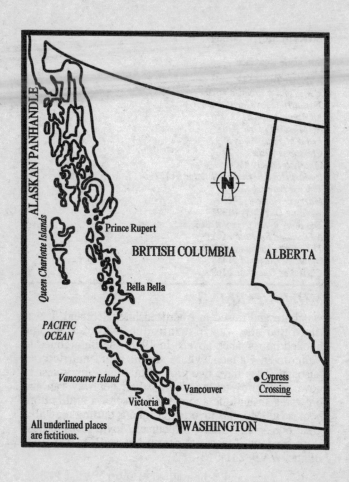

ALASKAN PANHANDLE

Queen Charlotte Islands

Prince Rupert

BRITISH COLUMBIA

ALBERTA

Bella Bella

PACIFIC
OCEAN

Vancouver Island

Cypress
Crossing

Victoria

Vancouver

All underlined places
are fictitious.

WASHINGTON

Chapter One

"You're too late. David's funeral was last week," said Eve Darling, recognizing the striking, dark-haired man from the photograph David Kingston had kept on his desk.

"I'm here now," he said, his expression guarded. Even so, Eve caught a hint of sadness in his gray eyes. David's death had hit her hard; he'd been her boss *and* her friend. How much harder must the loss be for David's brother?

"When you didn't answer my call, you left me no choice but to go ahead with the funeral arrangements," she said.

"I understand," he replied evenly. "What I need from you is the name and address of my brother's lawyer. The sooner I get his estate settled, the sooner I'll be able to leave."

At his words, shock rippled through Eve. No doubt David had left everything to his adopted brother. Could Mac Kingston have no interest in running the Kingston Inn, his brother's pride and joy?

How could two brothers be so different? David had been a warmhearted, generous man, loved by his staff and his neighbors in Cypress Crossing, a ski resort town in the interior of British Columbia.

The man gazing at her, dressed in a sheepskin jacket and blue jeans looked as if he'd walked off the cover of *GQ*. Was he really as unfeeling as he seemed?

David had always spoken proudly of his brother, but Mac Kingston had yet to live up to the glowing reviews, especially if his sole reason for coming to Cypress Crossing was to collect and dispose of his inheritance—the quicker the better.

With some effort, Eve clamped down on her anger. As much as she might want to tear a strip off the man, she had nothing to gain by making her feelings known.

Eve pushed herself to her feet and felt the baby, nestled beneath her heart, kick several times in protest.

"David's lawyer is Debra Graham. Her office is on Chestnut Drive, three blocks from here. She's been on holiday for the past three weeks."

"When is she expected back?"

Eve glanced at her desk calendar. "Today or to-morrow I believe."

"Would you call her office and find out?"

"Of course," she responded. Eve picked up the phone and punched in the number. After the third ring, much to Eve's surprise, Deb answered.

"Deb? Hi! You *are* back," she said. "Did you have a good holiday?" Eve listened to Deb's reply and felt her skin prickle with awareness of the man standing nearby, his impatience barely held in check.

"Listen, you've probably heard about David's death," Eve said. "Yes, it was a great shock," she acknowledged. "I know you must be busy catching up, but I wonder if you have a few minutes to spare. Mac Kingston, David's brother, has just arrived, and he's anxious to see you.

"Would it be all right if he came by your office now?" Eve asked, careful to avoid eye contact with the man on the other side of the desk.

"Sorry?" Distracted, she frowned, surprised by Deb's suggestion that she accompany Mac. "I can't at the moment," she said, unwilling to spend any more time with David's brother than she had to. "He'll be right over. Thanks, Deb. Talk to you soon."

"So Ms. Graham is back," Mac stated as she replaced the receiver.

Eve nodded. "And she can see you now."

"Did you say her office is on Chestnut Street?"

"Chestnut Drive," Eve corrected. "I'll write down the address for you."

Reaching across the desk, she retrieved a pad and pen. As she wrote, the fear and worry that had been her constant companions since David's unexpected death threatened to overwhelm her.

David had been a great boss and a true friend, agreeing to let her work right up until the birth, then return to her job as soon as she could make arrangements for day care.

She'd known David felt partly to blame for the predicament she'd found herself in. With no family of her own to turn to, he'd been the one who'd insisted she move into the basement suite of his luxury town house across from the inn.

Straightening, Eve held out the address.

As Mac Kingston took the slip of paper, his fingers brushed hers. The contact sent a jolt darting up her arm. Her gaze flew to meet his. Had he experienced the same strange sensation? she wondered. If he had, she could see no evidence of it in his eyes.

"I left my bag downstairs," he said. "The desk clerk told me the inn's full, but I believe my brother has a condo nearby."

"Yes, he does."

"Do you have a set of keys I can use?" he asked.

"They're right here." Eve opened the top drawer of her desk and brought out David's key ring.

"Actually, I should probably—" she began, about to tell him that for the past three months she'd rented the small suite of rooms in the basement of David's condo. But he didn't let her finish.

"Could you point me in the direction of the condo? I'll drop off my bag and continue to Ms. Graham's office."

"Of course."

Mac Kingston moved to open the office door. He stood waiting for her and, as Eve crossed the carpeted room, she was all too aware of his assessing gaze.

"How long had you worked for my brother?" he asked as they walked side by side to the stairs leading to the inn's main floor.

"Six years," she replied. "I've been the assistant manager for the past two years."

As they descended the stairs, the scent of pine from the eight-foot Christmas tree in the foyer mingled with the sweet smell of cinnamon and cloves.

The array of miniature, multicolored lights decorating the tree danced and flickered merrily. The festive feeling was enhanced by the familiar tones of a well-known Christmas carol being played on the piano in the lounge.

At the foot of the stairs Eve glanced through the French doors of the inn's cozy restaurant, pleased to note that almost all of the tables were occupied. At this time of year the majority of their guests were couples and groups of students enjoying their winter break. They came to the inn during the Christmas holidays for downhill skiing, snowboarding and cross-country skiing on a variety of groomed trails.

"Is the inn always this busy?" Mac asked as he stood aside to allow a group of young men to pass.

"During the Christmas season it is. We have a number of repeat guests who make reservations for next Christmas when they leave," Eve replied, pride in her voice.

Return business and regular customers played an important part in the success of the Kingston Inn. Since becoming the assistant manager she'd been working hard on new promotions, holiday packages and other incentives that would bring customers back again and again.

"Good…that should make it easier to sell the place."

At his words her feelings of pride and joy evaporated, leaving cold emptiness in their wake.

Eve stopped at the small window to the right of the inn's large oak door.

"David's condo is on the opposite corner. It's the one with the red and green Christmas lights outlining the roof," she said, pointing to the house at the end of the driveway and across the street. "You can't miss it. Perhaps I should—" she began in another attempt to tell him she lived in the basement suite.

"I'll manage," he assured her. "No doubt we'll talk again." With a nod of dismissal he strode toward the registration desk.

Eve stood staring after him. A shiver chased down her spine at the thought of his reaction when she showed up at the condo later.

Eager to put Mac from her mind and return to the quiet solitude of her office, she retraced her steps. The moment she opened the door lingering traces of his masculine scent assailed her, reminding her all too vividly of the man whose arrival in Cypress Crossing threatened to complicate her life.

Mac's comment about selling the inn replayed in her head. While a new owner would keep on the current housekeeping and restaurant staff, at least until they'd done an assessment of the workers, she doubted they would keep her on as assistant manager, not with a baby due in two weeks.

Tears pricked her eyes at the thought of leaving the job she loved.

And what about David's condo? No doubt it would be put on the market, too. A mixture of anger and despair washed over her at the realization that she would lose the temporary home David had generously provided.

With little money of her own, and the baby coming— Her thoughts broke off as the baby kicked her. Eve smiled and began, with slow circular motions, to gently massage her abdomen.

She pushed aside her troubled thoughts. According to her doctor and some of the books she'd read during the past eight months, fretting about the future or worrying about anything, for that matter, wasn't good for her unborn child.

Besides, she could be wrong. Maybe she had nothing to worry about. Maybe Mac Kingston wouldn't sell the inn after all. And maybe pigs would fly.

Mac dug in his pocket for David's keys, and after two tries, he succeeded in unlocking the door of his brother's condo.

The temptation to go inside and collapse onto a bed was strong, but he shook off the wave of exhaustion. His body was simply having trouble adjusting to the eight-hour time difference and the long flight from Zurich.

The doctors at the hospital in Interlaken hadn't wanted him to travel at all. They'd been reluctant to sign his release, pointing out that his dizzy spells were caused by the concussion he'd suffered while on a rescue mission. Two English students and one member of his team had died in an avalanche. He'd been lucky to suffer only bruises and a concussion when he'd been hurled down the mountainside.

Telling himself the dizziness would pass, he ignored the pain throbbing at his temples. Besides, David's lawyer was waiting for him, and he needed to deal with all the paperwork involved with his brother's death. Dropping his bag on the tiled floor just inside the condo, he pulled the door closed and retreated to the sidewalk.

He supposed the visit with David's lawyer could have waited till morning. David was dead, nothing could change that.

At the realization he would never see David again, pain clutched at Mac's heart. Not for the first time, he wished he'd been able to attend his brother's funeral. Eve's call had come several hours after he and his rescue team had set out in search of the missing skiers.

Guilt and regret sliced through him, and he felt tears sting his eyes. He blinked them away, refusing to allow his emotions to get the better of him. He'd learned at a very young age—while being bounced from foster home to foster home—to hide his feelings. That way he would never be vulnerable, never be weak, never be hurt.

He'd been thirteen and in trouble at school when he'd been sent to the Kingston family. Angry and rebellious, he'd long since given up his dream of being part of a family. That Christmas twenty-two years ago had changed his life forever. David's parents had taken Mac in, treated him like their own son and welcomed him into their family as if he truly belonged. For the first time in his life Mac had enjoyed the kind of Christmas every child dreams of.

David Kingston had been eighteen at the time, and Mac had braced himself for some sort of confrontation or bullying. But David had grinned, then punched Mac lightly on the arm before saying, "Wanna come to the ice rink with me and play hockey?"

Less than a year later the Kingstons adopted him. For five wonderful, happy, years he flourished under their love and acceptance. He'd begun to believe that *stupid* and *worthless*—labels he'd heard all of his life—didn't apply to him.

But when Maggie and Joe Kingston were killed in a car accident, his life had once more been thrown into chaos. In his grief and pain he'd withdrawn to that place where nothing and no one could hurt him. David had been his only connection to those happier times, and now he was gone, too.

Mac came to a halt at the traffic light and glanced at the street sign—Chestnut Drive. Turning right, he walked to the middle of the block. Debra Graham, Attorney at Law, was painted in black letters on an ornate oak door. With a twist of the brass doorknob he pushed it open.

The office appeared empty, but after a moment, a young woman with short black hair and a pixie face emerged from a room on his right.

"You must be Mac Kingston," she said as she

came toward him extending her hand. "I'm Debra Graham."

"Thank you for seeing me at such short notice," Mac replied as he shook her hand.

"Please come on in. Take off your jacket," she suggested as she retreated into the office. "First, let me say how sorry I am for your loss. David was a fine man and an asset to the community."

"Thank you," Mac mumbled as he shrugged out of his sheepskin jacket. Tossing it on one of the two chairs nearby, he sat down in the other.

"I must apologize for not contacting you sooner," Debra began. "I've been in Barbados on holiday and only returned this morning." She dropped into the leather chair behind her desk. "I was, in fact, in the process of writing to you," she said, patting the papers on her desk.

"Why don't you give me a brief rundown," Mac said. "I don't plan to spend any more time in Cypress Crossing than I absolutely have to. I'm anxious to get this business over with, to put the inn and David's condo on the market as soon as possible."

Debra leaned forward and clasped her hands together on the desktop.

"That might not be possible," she said.

Mac met her gaze with a puzzled frown. "I don't understand. I *am* David's only living relative."

"But not his only beneficiary."

"Go on."

"David left half of his estate to you and the other half to Eve Darling."

Chapter Two

The temperature had dropped several degrees below zero by the time Eve approached the front door of the condo. She pulled off a glove and fumbled in her coat pocket for her keys. Before sliding the key into the lock she hesitated, wondering if David's brother had returned from his visit to Debra Graham's office.

Stepping into the welcome warmth of the hallway, she almost tripped over the soft-sided bag sitting on the floor. Mac Kingston hadn't returned. With a sharp sense of relief, Eve closed the outer door and crossed the entryway to her small suite. Since David's death she'd avoided going upstairs, having difficulty coming to terms with the loss of her friend.

She blinked back tears that were never far from the surface these days and entered her suite. She shrugged out of her coat, hung it in her closet and let out a soft groan of protest as she leaned against the wall to remove her boots. Sliding her feet into an old pair of slippers, she remembered she hadn't checked the mailbox.

She returned to the outer door and was greeted by an icy gust of wind. As she removed several envelopes from the mailbox, a deep voice startled her.

"What the hell do you think you're doing?"

The letters slid from her grasp to fall like giant pieces of confetti at Mac Kingston's feet.

"You're back," Eve said.

Mac bent to gather up the envelopes before meeting her gaze. "Moved in already, I see."

Hearing the derision in his voice, Eve frowned. "I tried to tell you earlier that David and I had an arrangement—"

"I just bet you did." His sarcasm cut short her explanation. He took a step toward her forcing her to retreat. She just managed to sidestep the bag on the floor.

"I live in the basement suite. David insisted," she hurried on.

"Really?" Mac elbowed the outer door closed behind him, challenge in every line of his body.

Eve bristled. "I'm not sure what you're implying.

David kindly offered me his basement suite as a temporary measure until the baby is born.''

"How generous," Mac said dryly as he tucked the letters inside his jacket.

"Yes," Eve agreed. "David had a reputation for being both kind and generous." She wished she knew why Mac's steely gaze made her feel as if she'd just crawled out from under a rock. "I am paying rent," she assured him.

But if Eve thought her announcement would extinguish the animosity burning in his eyes, she was mistaken. "If the arrangement doesn't suit you, I'll start looking for other accommodations tomorrow."

"We both know that's not necessary," he said as he bent down to pick up his bag.

"Not necessary?" Eve repeated. "I don't understand. Are you saying I can stay?"

Mac straightened to his full height, forcing Eve to look up at him. Eyes the color of a stormy sea stared back at her.

"That's very good," he said with sarcasm. "You don't really expect me to believe you don't know."

"Know what?" Bewilderment echoed through her voice.

"That my brother left you half of everything he owned!"

Shock slammed into her with the force of a speeding train. She stumbled back and might have fallen if not for Mac's lightning reflexes. Dropping his bag, he grabbed her arm and pulled her toward him.

When her rounded belly bumped him she froze. Her gaze darted to meet his, and for a second an emotion she couldn't decipher glinted in his eyes.

She could feel the warmth of his breath fanning her face, and where their bodies touched a scorching heat radiated through her. Her pulse leaped crazily, and the baby reacted, too, kicking her abdomen in obvious agitation.

Mac inhaled sharply. His gaze dropped to where the baby's repeated kicks made Eve's maternity top dance. He stared at the spot for several long seconds before releasing her. Scooping up his bag once more, he turned and headed for the stairs.

Eve retreated into her rooms. Leaning against the closed door she waited for the erratic beat of her heart to slow down. She tried to assure herself that her reaction had nothing to do with Mac Kingston and everything to do with the fact that in the final month of her pregnancy the smallest exertion could result in breathlessness or an accelerated pulse.

Clinging to that feeble rationale, she made her way to her small kitchen where her thoughts shifted to Mac's startling announcement. Was it true? Had David really left her half of everything he'd owned?

"Oh, David." Her voice trembled and tears stung her eyes. She was deeply moved that he'd thought to mention her in his will.

Undoubtedly that was the reason Deb Graham had wanted Eve to come to the office. But Eve had been too intent on getting rid of Mac to question the request. She tugged a tissue from the box on the kitchen counter and blew her nose.

If David had left her half of all he owned, surely Deb would have notified her? Except that Deb had left for her holiday before David died, and she'd only just returned.

Her thoughts in a jumble, Eve filled the kettle and set it on the stove. As she prepared a tray, the phrase "half of everything" echoed inside her head. Had David really left her such a generous legacy?

He'd done so much for her already, letting her stay in the basement for minimal rent and helping her come to terms with the fact that she would soon be raising a child on her own.

She hadn't intended to confide her troubles to David, but when he'd come upon her weeping in her office, she'd blurted out the whole sordid story.

David had introduced her to Larry Dawson almost a year ago. An old friend from high school, Larry had come to Cypress Crossing on business. A real estate developer, he'd been checking out the area for some clients.

Larry, with his brash good looks, outgoing personality and easy charm, had swept her off her feet. And like a besotted fool she'd believed him when, at the end of their first dinner date, he'd told her he was in grave danger of falling in love with her.

For the next two weeks he sent her flowers every day and took her to dinner every night. She'd been easy prey for a man like Larry, who seduced her with vague hints of a future together.

He'd told her all about the real estate deal he was working on, inviting her to invest her savings, saying he could triple her money in only a few months.

At first she'd been unwilling to take the risk, but her doubts were erased when Larry told her David had bought into the deal. She'd gone to the bank, had a certified check drawn up and handed her savings over to Larry.

The next morning he was gone, leaving a trail of unpaid bills and broken promises. The real estate deal had been a scam, and while she hadn't been the only person in town who'd lost money, when she realized she was pregnant, she knew she'd been the biggest fool of all.

After her confession, David, who hadn't invested in the deal after all, began to make some discreet inquiries about his old friend. He'd discovered Larry not only had a wife, but there were a variety of outstanding warrants for his arrest for theft and fraud.

A short, sharp knock on her door drove away her thoughts of Larry.

It had to be Mac. Her heart skipped a beat, and

for one moment she entertained the thought of ignoring him. The knock came again. Taking a deep, steadying breath she crossed to open the door.

"Yes?"

His tall figure filled the doorway, and Eve couldn't help noticing that his black polo sweater, tucked into his jeans, fitted his muscled shoulders and chest like a glove.

"Ms. Graham asked me to give you this." He held out an envelope.

"Thank you," she said. As she took the letter from his outstretched hand she saw the grimace of pain that flitted across his features and noticed for the first time the shadows under his eyes that spoke of fatigue.

Behind her the kettle on the stove began to whistle.

"I'm making tea. Would you like a cup?" she asked, surprising herself with the invitation.

He hesitated, but only for a moment. "Thank you."

She'd expected him to brush aside her invitation and, in truth, she'd hoped he would. Perhaps being upstairs in his brother's house, where there were numerous reminders of David's presence, had stirred some emotion in him.

Eve dropped the envelope on the kitchen counter and turned off the stove. "Do you take milk and sugar?"

"Just milk." He'd followed her into the small living area and now he stood on the other side of the counter. "There isn't much in the way of food upstairs."

"If you'd let me know you were coming I would have brought in some groceries." She added a second cup and saucer to the tray.

"I didn't think about it...I just came."

At the bleak tone of his voice Eve glanced at him and watched as he closed his eyes and pinched the bridge of his nose.

"Do you have a headache?" she asked, sympathy in her voice.

Cautiously his eyes met hers. "Yes, I do."

"Would you like an aspirin?" Eve asked, placing the teapot on the tray.

"I've already taken my medication. It hasn't kicked in yet," he told her. "Let me get that," he added as he reached for the tray.

Eve came around the counter, wondering at his remark about medication, but she refrained from commenting.

Mac set the tray on the coffee table.

"Please sit down," she invited. A shiver of relief danced through her when he chose the armchair at the opposite end of the coffee table. She sank onto the small love seat and sighed audibly as she brought her legs around to stretch out in front of her.

"When's your baby due?"

"In about two weeks."

"And you're still working?" She heard the censure in his voice.

"I didn't see any point quitting work to sit around and wait for the baby to arrive. David agreed," she replied.

"You and my brother appear to have had a close relationship," Mac commented.

"We were friends as well as colleagues," she said, noting the glint of skepticism in his glance.

"Is that all?"

"Yes, that's all," Eve replied, an edge to her tone, knowing exactly what he was implying.

"Are you saying that David isn't the father of your baby?"

Eve inhaled sharply, fighting to keep her anger in check. She met his challenging gaze head on.

"That's right. He isn't the baby's father," she responded, her tone even.

"In view of the fact he's left you half of everything he owned, I find that hard to believe."

"David and I were friends, nothing more." Her words only served to bring a smile to his face, a smile that didn't reach his eyes.

"Ms. Graham told me David changed his will two months ago," Mac went on. "When did you move in here?"

Eve felt blood rush to her cheeks, but she refused

to let him intimidate her. She held his gaze. "Three months ago," Eve said, aware of his fleeting smile of satisfaction.

"Tell me again he isn't the baby's father," he invited.

"I'm not lying. David isn't the baby's father," she repeated, but her voice wavered. She reached for the teapot.

"Allow me." Mac proceeded to fill both cups. He held one out to Eve. "If David isn't the father, who is?"

Shock at his rudeness brought the anger she'd been trying to suppress bubbling to the surface. Defiantly now, she faced him.

"I don't see that the identity of my baby's father is any of your business." This time a glimmer of respect danced briefly in his eyes, but she sensed he still wasn't convinced.

She accepted the cup and saucer he held out and sat back against the cushions. Her moment of triumph was short-lived as her hands began to shake uncontrollably, spilling tea into her saucer.

"Careful!" Mac reached out to steady her trembling hands.

At the contact Eve froze. For several breathstealing seconds their gazes locked. She refused to look away, determined not to give him the satisfaction.

He released her and stood up, but not before she

glimpsed a look of sorrow in his eyes. "I think I'll pass on the tea after all."

"Fine," Eve replied, relieved he was leaving.

Halfway to the door he stopped and turned around. "By the way, along with the letter I gave you from Ms. Graham, you'll find a copy of David's will."

Eve waited for the sound of the door to close before releasing the breath she'd been holding.

Hands still shaking, she brought the cup to her lips. The tea was lukewarm but she drank it down, refusing to think about the sadness she'd seen in his eyes.

She rose and carried the tray of dishes to the sink. Picking up the envelope, she opened it and read the contents confirming the generous legacy David had left to her and her baby.

Eve hugged the letter to her and blinked back tears once more. She supposed Mac had every right to be angry. He'd come to Cypress Crossing to quickly dispose of David's assets and return to Switzerland.

By leaving her half of everything, David had thrown a wrench in the works. And though Mac's question concerning the identity of her baby's father was rude, she understood his reason for asking it.

She doubted he'd believed her denial, but she wasn't about to confess to a stranger that she'd made a complete fool of herself over a worthless con man.

David's generosity was more than she deserved, but she refused to feel guilty, regardless of whether or not Mac approved of his brother's decision. David had discussed his dreams for the inn countless times, especially his plans for the new piece of property he'd bought a few months ago.

He wanted to build a golf course and clubhouse on the new property, and Eve vowed to do everything in her power to see David's plans and dreams fulfilled.

Eve spent a restless night, her mind filled with a mixture of excitement and fear. Excitement at the thought of how she would execute David's plans and fear of the added responsibilities now resting on her shoulders. Not even the knowledge that she was in a partnership with Mac Kingston could extinguish the joy and relief of knowing her future was secure.

She turned on the shower and stood under the warm spray. Her back ached and had done so for the better part of the night. Her due date was Christmas Eve, two weeks away. Right now that seemed like an eternity.

The baby prodded her, as if in agreement, and Eve smiled. "Yes, I know you're anxious to set foot in the world."

When she'd first learned of her pregnancy, the prospect of having a baby had thrilled her, but reality quickly set in, along with a bundle of doubts and fears. David had been the one who'd helped her come to terms with becoming a single parent. And while Larry's treatment of her had left a bitter taste in her mouth and a scar on her heart, she'd quickly realized her baby was a gift to be cherished and loved.

Eve stepped out of the shower, dried herself and dressed in one of her favorite outfits, a cobalt-blue maternity top and matching slacks. With deft strokes she swept her hair into a tidy French roll and applied a minimum of makeup. As she stared at her reflection, she had to admit she was looking forward to wearing "normal" clothes again.

She skipped her morning cup of herbal tea and pulled on her boots and overcoat. With gloves in hand she patted her pocket to make sure she hadn't forgotten her keys and wallet.

At the door leading to the communal entranceway, she hesitated. She knew Mac was up and about because she'd heard the upstairs shower running. And while she acknowledged it was foolish to avoid him, she didn't feel up to dealing with his cool arrogance this early in the morning. Squaring her shoulders she opened the door a crack and peeked out, relieved to find the entranceway empty.

Eve hurried across to the outer door. Once on the sidewalk, she pulled on her gloves, noting the fresh layer of snow that had fallen during the night. It was still dark out, and the air felt crisp and cold.

She loved this time of morning when she seemed to have the whole world to herself. With some caution she navigated to the street corner, and when the traffic light changed in her favor, she carefully made her way across.

As she approached the pedestrian walkway leading to the inn she stopped, surprised to note that the students she'd hired to clear the walkways around the inn hadn't done their job. She made a mental note to call maintenance as soon as she reached her office.

Eve contemplated her options. She could tackle the walkway in the hope no ice had formed beneath the newly fallen snow, or she could skirt the snow piled in the gutter and use the driveway.

"Need any help?"

Eve felt her heart career against her breastbone. She didn't have to turn around to know Mac was right behind her. Preoccupied with her dilemma she hadn't heard his approach.

"Ah, thanks...I can manage." Anxious to put some distance between them, she decided to take her chances on the snow-covered walkway, but when she moved forward she felt her boot slide on the ice.

Mac put his arm around her, and Eve had no option but to lean against him until she regained her footing.

"Let's get you safely inside, shall we?"

Keeping his arm around her back, he grasped her

gloved hand and guided her up the walkway. Once inside she turned to thank him, and as their gazes collided, the air between them crackled and an unexpected warmth suffused her body. Whenever Mac came anywhere near her, her whole body reacted. What was it about him that affected her so dramatically?

Determined not to let him see her reaction, she held his gaze and again saw sorrow lingering in the silvery depths of his eyes.

"I don't know about you, but I'm starving," Mac commented as he released her. "I assume the restaurant serves breakfast."

"Of course," Eve responded.

"Care to join me?"

The invitation surprised her. She'd planned to pick up a muffin and juice and take it to her office. "I really should get upstairs…" she began.

"Have you eaten?"

"No. I—"

"You shouldn't skip breakfast," he said. "Besides, we need to talk."

"About what?" Eve asked, suddenly wary.

"I have a proposition for you."

Chapter Three

"A proposition?" Eve repeated and felt a quiver of alarm chase down her spine.

"A business proposition," Mac replied, and at his words Eve's heart sank. Larry had used the exact same phrase when he'd talked her into investing in his real estate project, and that had proved disastrous.

"Won't you hear me out?" A slow smile spread over his features sending her pulse tripping.

"I really—" she began.

"It won't take long," he assured her.

"All right."

Magda, the hostess, greeted them with a welcoming smile. "Good morning. Two for breakfast?"

"Please," Eve replied, aware of the speculative

look in the other girl's eyes. "Oh, and if anyone is looking for me—"

"I'll tell them where to find you," Magda finished with a smile, before leading the way to a table by the window. "Coffee, sir?"

"Please." He removed his jacket and hung it over the back of his chair.

"And would you like lemon or raspberry tea this morning?" Magda asked, when Eve was seated.

"Lemon, please," she replied.

Magda gave them each a menu. "Your waitress will be right over with your beverages and to take your order," she said before withdrawing.

Eve pretended to peruse the menu. He'd said he had a proposition. Had he spent the night trying to think of a way to divest her of her half of David's legacy? She'd soon know.

Through lowered lashes she studied his handsome face, noting the faint lines of strain near his mouth. Her gaze lingered on his full, sensual lips, and, to her surprise, a tingling heat spread through her.

Annoyed, she set the menu aside.

"Tell me about this proposition," she said, deciding on a direct approach.

"I want to buy you out."

"Buy me out?" she repeated, unable to hide her surprise. "Why on earth would I want to sell?"

"Because you're going to have a baby in two weeks. Selling would give you enough money to live on and allow you freedom from all the responsibilities that come with owning and running an inn. And, of course, I'd make it worth your while. Give you a fair price. What do you say?'' He held her gaze, his cool gray eyes boring into hers, silently urging her to agree.

She swallowed, but it did nothing to alleviate the sudden dryness in her throat.

''It was coffee for you, sir, and lemon tea here.'' The waitress's cheery voice cut through the silence as she set the cup and teapot on the table in front of Eve.

Eve pulled her gaze away from Mac's. ''Thanks, Sally,'' she murmured, grateful for the distraction. She reached for the teapot and quickly filled her cup.

As soon as the waitress took their orders and withdrew, Mac picked up exactly where he'd left off. ''Take a few days and think about it. You don't have to give me your answer now.'' He took a sip of coffee.

Eve drew a steadying breath. ''I'm not interested in selling,'' she said, pleased that her voice sounded firm and unwavering. His mouth tightened with irritation, and she vowed to stick to her guns.

''That's a gut reaction and I understand it, believe me,'' he went on, lowering his cup. ''Take my advice, think seriously about my offer.''

''I don't need your advice,'' she told him, keeping her tone even while anger churned within her. ''And

I don't need time to think things through. I'm not interested in selling my share of David's estate to you or to anyone."

"We remain partners then," he said easily, annoying her further with his calm acceptance. "Unless you can buy me out." His voice trailed off suggestively, and Eve glimpsed what she thought might be a smile teasing the corner of his mouth.

The sharp tug at her senses surprised her. Was he smiling or sneering? She couldn't be sure. Damn the man! Before she could think of a cutting response, the waitress appeared with their breakfasts.

"Here we are." After setting their plates in front of them, the waitress topped off Mac's coffee from the carafe she carried. "Enjoy," she said before scurrying away.

Mac picked up his fork and proceeded to eat the scrambled eggs, hash browns and toast he'd ordered. Eve cut her muffin into bite-size pieces and popped one into her mouth.

"Ms. Graham told me about the acreage David bought recently. Where exactly is it? Have you seen it?" he asked as he munched on a piece of toast.

"David took me out to see the property the day he bought it."

"And...?"

"Oh...it's a beautiful piece of land," Eve told him, recalling how David hadn't been able to contain his excitement, chattering all the way there about the great plans he had for it.

"The last time I spoke to David he didn't mention it. Did he have a specific reason for buying the land?"

"Yes," she replied. "He thought it would make an ideal location for a golf course and clubhouse."

A flicker of interest brightened his gray eyes. "Sounds ambitious."

"The inn doesn't do as much business during the summer months," she explained. "David thought a golf course would bring in more tourists and turn the inn into a year-round destination."

"I see," Mac spoke softly. "And drawing up the plans would have been right up David's alley."

Eve heard the sorrow vibrating in his voice and wondered if beneath Mac's abrasive shell lurked a man who kept his emotions locked up tight.

"How far out of town is this place?" he asked suddenly.

"Thirty-five miles or so."

"Where is David's car? I assume he has one."

"He has a truck with four-wheel drive," she told him. "It's parked in the lot behind the inn. Why?"

"I'd like to drive out to the property and take a look around."

"The truck keys are upstairs in David's office," Eve said, thinking that with Mac out of the way for a few hours, her day might not turn out too badly after all. "I'll get them for you and draw you a map," she offered.

"I won't need a map." He pushed his empty plate away.

"You won't?" Eve frowned.

His steady gaze held hers. "No, because you're coming with me."

A shiver raced through her at the thought of spending any more time with him. "Sorry, I have work to do."

"From what I've seen this place pretty well runs itself. I don't think they'd miss you for a few hours." He rose and, digging his hand into his trouser pocket, withdrew a handful of bills.

"But, I really—" she began.

"As half owner of the land, I think it's only right we tour it together," he cut in. "What do you say?"

Eve opened her mouth to say exactly what she thought, but bit back the retort. "All right, I'll go with you," she replied.

The smile that tugged at the corner of his mouth did strange things to her heart.

"Good. I'll meet you in your office around one o'clock," he said. "That should give you ample time to arrange for someone to keep an eye on things here. You do know how to delegate, don't you?" He tossed several bills on the table and grabbed his coat. "In the meantime I'm going to do a little exploring. I'll see you at one."

Without waiting for a reply he turned on his heel and strode out of the restaurant, leaving Eve to glare after him in frustration.

Eve glanced for the hundredth time at the clock on her desk. The digital numbers said one-fifteen but Mac still hadn't appeared. Part of her felt relieved, while another part of her began to worry.

She'd returned to her office after breakfast and had quickly become caught up in her daily tasks. Most of the morning had been spent on paperwork, but she'd also been called away to deal with a disgruntled guest and a minor squabble in the kitchen.

After settling both matters, she'd ordered a sandwich and taken it back to her office. It was satisfying to know that for the third year in a row, the inn was fully booked until early in the New Year. Not for the first time she wished David were there to acknowledge and celebrate the inn's success.

A light tap on her office door brought her out of her reverie, and she looked up to see Mac standing in the doorway. His black hair fell in disarray over his forehead, and at the sight of him her heart gave a lurch. From the look of his red cheeks he'd spent some time outside in the chill.

"Ready to go?" he asked without preamble.

"Yes, but I really don't think—" Eve began.

"Good!" He jumped in. "I'll drive. You can tell me where to go." He flashed her a smile that sent her pulse skyrocketing. "Let me rephrase that. You can be the navigator. Where are the keys? And more important, where is the truck?"

Eve put on her coat and gloves and led the way to the parking lot at the rear of the inn. Mac had been right when he'd said the inn practically ran itself. The well-trained staff could be relied on to take care of most problems. But just in case anyone asked, she'd told the receptionist and cook she would be out for the rest of the day.

They were soon settled in the truck's cab and heading down Main Street. A few miles out of town Eve directed Mac to make the turn that would take them to the road leading to the cabin. The terrain changed, and they began to climb.

When she'd made this same journey with David back in early October the roads had been dry and clear and it had taken them only a little more than forty minutes. But the current snowy conditions slowed the trip considerably.

Eve said little throughout the drive, content to enjoy the beauty of the snowy landscape gradually unfolding before them. They might have been the only two people in the world for they didn't encounter any vehicles.

Mac proved to be a competent driver, negotiating the winding curves and steady climb with the ease and confidence of someone accustomed to driving in snowy conditions.

Eve shifted in her seat in an attempt to ease the persistent ache in her back, an ache she'd been trying unsuccessfully to ignore all morning.

Earlier she'd checked the weather forecast and been told a cold front and storm were approaching, but snowfall wasn't due until late in the evening.

Looking at the gray clouds gathering in the sky above and the tiny white flakes already beginning to fall, Eve suspected the storm had other plans.

"There's the cabin," Eve said shortly after they'd made the left turn. Up ahead, through the clump of trees, she caught sight of the rustic building, its roof already laden with snow.

"David told me the property originally belonged to a man named Abe Kirkland," she went on. "He once owned the hardware store in town. When he retired ten years ago he sold his house and moved out here. There's not much in the way of neighboring houses or cabins and he became a bit of a recluse. He died a year ago leaving the property to his brother." She stopped as Mac pulled the truck into the snowbank at the edge of the road.

"I'll walk to the cabin and have a quick look around," he said. "Want to join me?"

She shook her head. "I'll wait here."

"I won't be long," he said. "By the look of those clouds it's going to start snowing in earnest soon."

"I think you're right," she acknowledged. "Oh,

if you want to take a look inside there's a key hidden under the granite rock to the left of the door.''

"Okay. I'll leave the engine running and the heater on," he said before climbing out.

"Thanks," Eve replied, warmed by his thoughtfulness.

She watched Mac move around the front of the truck and wade through the two-foot-deep snow that covered the driveway leading to the cabin.

Her gaze drifted past him to the landscape beyond, its stark beauty casting a spell on her just as it had done when she and David had made the journey.

Now half of this property belonged to her. She shook her head, still having difficulty believing her good fortune. Her thoughts turned to David and his dream of a golf course and clubhouse. Somehow she had to find a way to make it come true.

Tears blurred her vision, and she blinked them away. She didn't want Mac to return and find her crying. Eve shifted in her seat, trying to ease the nagging ache in her back.

Nothing worked. Undoubtedly she'd been sitting in the truck too long. Maybe if she stood up and stretched her legs for a few minutes it would help. Releasing her seat belt, she reached over to turn off the engine before opening the passenger door.

She shivered as icy fingers of wind chilled the air. Easing out of the cab, she stood up in the snow. She left the truck door open as she moved away. Pressing her hands against the small of her back she twisted from side to side in the faint hope of finding some relief, but the ache persisted.

Seconds later she felt a rush of wetness cascade down her thighs. She gasped in astonishment, realizing what had happened. Turning, she reached for the door handle, but her knees buckled, and she toppled like a felled tree into the snowbank.

Chapter Four

Mac trudged through the snow toward the covered porch. He could see the cabin had been built with long cedar logs that sat atop each other in simple perfection.

Someone had done a beautiful job, he thought, as he reached the front door. His gaze shifted to the snow-covered valley and the trees and mountains rising up on either side. The view reminded him a little of the Alps, and, staring across the vast landscape dotted here and there with tall cedars, he understood the potential David had seen.

Large snowflakes were beginning to fall from the gray, cloud-laden sky. A quick look around would have to suffice, he thought, at least for now. Locating the key hidden under the rock, he unlocked the door.

Once inside, the strong scent of cedar and dust assailed him. The spacious living room had a granite fireplace, blackened by use, and a number of rustic pieces of furniture, including an old sofa and matching reclining chair.

Shelves filled with books and magazines dotted the perimeter, and suddenly he could see David relaxing in the chair in front of the fire. A feeling of grief slammed into him with the realization that he would never again see his adopted brother, would never again enjoy David's company or the friendship they'd forged over the years.

He hadn't found out about his brother's death until after he'd been released from the hospital. He'd listened to the message over and over, but the reality hadn't sunk in.

A cavalcade of memories began to play in his mind, and he felt his throat tighten with emotion. Mac closed his eyes against the sting of tears, fighting to rein in the wave of grief threatening to overwhelm him.

Inhaling deeply, he squared his shoulders and, turning on his heel, headed down the hall. After a brief glance around the kitchen, he retreated and poked his head into the two rooms located on opposite sides of the hall.

One was a bathroom, the other a bedroom with a double bed and mirrored dressing table. An old wicker chair was stationed to the right of the door

and on a table next to the bed sat a Tiffany-
style lamp.

He crossed to the window that overlooked the rear
of the property. Visibility had decreased considerably, and, the snow fell thick and fast. Surprised by
how quickly the weather had deteriorated, Mac returned to the front door. As he pulled it closed he
cast a quick glance toward the truck, noticing that
the passenger door stood open. Frowning, he peered
through the falling snowflakes in search of Eve.

His gaze shifted to a dark shape lying on the
snowbank next to the truck. When he saw an arm
being raised he realized, with a start, the figure was
Eve.

The cabin forgotten, Mac bolted off the porch.

Eve tried to ignore the icy wetness trickling down
her neck as she lay on her side in the snow. The
pain that had gripped her abdomen moments after
she fell had subsided but she couldn't seem to find
the strength to stand up.

The sensation of being squeezed like an orange
had been too intense for a cramp and she knew without a doubt she'd experienced her first contraction.
She was in labor!

Eve lifted her arm and tried to get up, but her
efforts proved futile. She sank deeper into the snow,
then whimpered in fear and frustration.

"Are you all right?" Mac's anxious question

brought her attention to the man bending over her. He didn't wait for a reply, but slid his hand around her, gently easing her into a sitting position.

Eve saw concern on his face.

"What happened?" he asked.

"I thought I'd stretch my legs," she explained. "But when I stepped out of the truck my water broke. I'm in labor."

Shock registered on his handsome features. "We'd better get you to a hospital."

Fear and panic licked at the edges of Eve's mind. What if they didn't make it into town in time? What if the roads were already slippery thanks to the freshly falling snow? What if the truck got stranded halfway to town?

Mac levered her onto her feet, but before he could take one step toward the truck she felt as if her stomach was being clamped in a vise.

"Oooh!" Eve put her hand on her abdomen in a protective gesture. "It's another contraction." Her breath hitched as pain overtook her, robbing her of coherent thought. She closed her eyes and tightened her grip on Mac's hand.

Eve leaned into him, and he braced himself struggling to keep them both upright. He held on to her and watched as she valiantly coped with the contraction racking her body.

Minutes passed, minutes when the falling snow began to form a thin layer on their clothing, minutes when Mac silently berated himself for insisting Eve accompany him.

"Is it over?" he asked when her breathing eased and her grip on his hand relaxed fractionally.

She nodded, still fighting for breath.

"Can you make it to the truck?" Mac asked.

"I'm not sure that's a good idea," Eve's voice wavered a little.

"We need to get you to a hospital."

"There isn't time."

Startled, Mac met her gaze. "What do you mean?"

"My baby's in a hurry to be born."

"I thought babies took hours to arrive," he countered.

"Sometimes they do."

"But not this one," he commented wryly.

Eve shook her head.

"The only other option is the cabin," Mac said. "It's a bit dusty inside but it's dry and relatively comfortable. Once I get you settled I'll call an ambulance. There is a phone inside, isn't there?" he asked, though he couldn't recall seeing one during his tour.

"I'm afraid not," Eve said. "The previous owner liked his privacy and didn't have one installed. David brought his cell phone with him when he came, but the reception in this area is sporadic at the best of times. He figured it had something to do with the surrounding mountains. At any rate I didn't bring the phone with me,'' she confessed, annoyed that she hadn't even thought about it.

The knowledge that they couldn't contact the medical services Eve required made Mac hesitate. He turned and glanced first at the truck then at the cabin, both were already scarcely visible. "Let's get you inside,'' he said decisively.

He scooped Eve into his arms and trudged through the snow toward the cabin. Nudging the door open, he carried her straight through to the bedroom, oblivious to the trail of melting snow following in his wake.

With great care he lowered her onto the quilted bedspread. Then, tossing his gloves on the bed, he knelt on the floor and proceeded to tug off Eve's wet gloves before undoing the buttons on her coat.

He managed to remove her coat, dropping it on the chair by the door. After adjusting the pillows behind her back for support, he stood up to leave, but Eve reached out to capture his arm.

"Don't go,'' she pleaded, and when he met her gaze he saw the fear and anxiety clouding her blue eyes.

"I'm not going anywhere,'' he assured her. He shrugged out of his jacket, throwing it on top of hers, then sat down on the edge of the bed, taking her hand in his.

"Thank you,'' Eve managed to say.

Suddenly her grip on his hand tightened to such a degree he thought his fingers might break. He watched beads of perspiration form on her forehead as she rode the wave of pain.

She stared straight into his eyes, but he didn't think she really saw him. Her breath came out in sharp, controlled bursts and when several strands of her dark brown hair tumbled loose to fall across her face, he reached up to gently tuck them behind her ear.

A few minutes later, when her grip on his fingers slowly relaxed and her breathing returned to a semblance of normal, he knew the powerful contraction had ended. She fell back against the pillows.

"I'm sorry. I hope I didn't hurt you." She released his hand.

"That was pretty intense," Mac commented. "Any idea how long it will be before the baby comes?"

Eve shook her head, causing the remainder of her hair caught up in hairpins to break free and cascade around her shoulders.

Mac stared at the chocolate-colored curls framing a face that even under duress looked both beautiful and vulnerable.

"I have a little medical training," he told her. "But I've never been present at a birth."

"Neither have I," Eve said, and Mac saw the glint of humor in her eyes.

"I'll put some water on to boil." He stood up. "That's what they do in the movies," he said with a grin. "And I'll see if I can find some towels. Once the baby arrives we'll need to keep him or her warm. Is there anything I can do to make you more comfortable?"

"I'd love a glass of water," she replied, wondering what he meant by some medical training.

"I'll be right back," he said, before she could ask him.

After Mac had gone, Eve tried to quash the fear threatening to resurface. She berated herself once more for not bringing David's cell phone with her. This wasn't supposed to happen. She was supposed to be in the hospital, with a trained medical staff around her, not in a cabin in the middle of nowhere caught in a snowstorm.

She glanced down at her wet and rather bedraggled state. She needed to remove her clothes. She listened for a moment for Mac returning but heard nothing. Easing herself over to the edge of the bed she slid off her slacks and underwear and kicked them aside. Before lying back on the pillows, she pulled the blanket folded at the bottom of the bed over her.

The previous contraction had been strong, and she'd been aware of her stomach muscles working to push the baby down the birth canal. She tried to remember what she'd read about the timing of contractions. How long would it be before she felt the urge to push?

And what if something went wrong? The question sent a ripple of anxiety through her. Maybe they should have gone in the truck after all.

Eve drew a steadying breath, telling herself over and over again she had no reason to panic. After all, childbirth was a normal and natural occurrence. Women had been giving birth for centuries, and more often than not without the assistance of doctors and nurses.

Her thoughts shifted to the nagging backache that had plagued her throughout the previous night and most of the morning. That must have been when her labor started.

The sound of footsteps told her Mac was returning. When he appeared in the doorway the feeling of relief that swept over her surprised her. Mac seemed to be taking everything in stride. He hadn't panicked. He'd stayed with her. No doubt that had something to do with the medical training he'd mentioned. But just his very presence had helped immeasurably.

She knew of several men, David included, who would have reacted to the situation in an entirely different way. They'd have argued with her when she'd told them they wouldn't make it to town in time, or ignored her protests, putting her in the truck and driving away without a thought to the possible dangers of such an action.

Mac had done neither. He'd accepted her assessment and acted accordingly.

"Here we are." He dropped an armful of towels on the foot of the bed before handing her a glass of water.

"Thanks." She took several sips, enjoying the coolness trickling down her throat before setting the glass on the bedside table.

"How long until the next contraction?"

"A couple of minutes maybe." She smiled feebly.

"Don't suppose you've looked outside," he said. "But the wind is really starting to blow and visibility is down to zero. The storm is hitting us full force." He nodded toward the window. "I doubt we'd have gotten far if we'd tried to drive back to town."

Eve followed his gaze to the swirling snow outside and shivered at the thought of being stranded in the truck in freezing temperatures. At least here they would be warm and dry and safe from the storm.

She gasped as another contraction gripped her.

Mac crossed to the bed and after a quick glance at his watch took her hand in his.

"Easy, now. Take deep breaths. That's right. You're doing fine." He repeated the phrases, his deep voice offering encouragement and comfort at the same time.

As Eve listened, she remembered her instructor telling her that to stay focused she should look directly into the eyes of her birthing coach.

Eve met Mac's steady, unflinching gaze. As their eyes locked she felt his strength and confidence flow into her, enabling her to suppress the fear and panic threatening to take hold.

Keeping her attention on Mac, on the power behind his steel-gray eyes, she found the strength to ignore the almost overpowering need to push, instinctively knowing it was too soon. When the contraction at last ebbed, she fell back against the pillows, exhausted.

"That contraction lasted nearly five minutes," he told her. "They're certainly intense, and if that's anything to go by, I'd say this baby's in one heck of a hurry to be born." Mac released her hand and stood up.

"Are you sure you've never done this before?" Eve asked.

"Never."

"You said something about having medical training," she went on. "I thought David said you were the owner of a hostel in the Swiss Alps."

"I am," he confirmed. "I'm also a member of the local mountain rescue team. We're required to keep our first-aid skills up-to-date, and that means taking refresher classes every couple of years.''

''I see,'' Eve said, intrigued by this revelation. ''Do you get called out often?'' she asked, finding the conversation a welcome distraction.

''It depends,''. he replied. ''We're usually called out to rescue injured skiers or locate lost ones. Or there are those fools on the slopes who have no respect for the mountains and who think skiing out-of-bounds is a challenge…until they get lost or hurt.'' Anger laced his voice.

''That happens here, too,'' Eve said. ''We've even had a few avalanches lately. I suppose you get your share of those.''

At her words Eve saw the color drain from Mac's face. Before she could pursue the subject further, another contraction stole her breath.

For the next half hour the contractions bombarded her, leaving little reprieve. When the urge to push transcended everything, Eve bore down with all her might.

The silence that followed seemed to last an eternity. Then her baby's cry pierced the stillness. Her heart leaped at the incredible sound, and tears of wonder and relief blurred her vision.

''Is the baby all right?'' she asked, a hint of tension in her voice.

''She's perfect,'' Mac replied hoarsely. ''Hold on

a minute.'' After gently wiping the baby's head and face, he carefully wrapped her in a clean towel.

Mac gazed in silent wonder at the tiny infant he'd helped bring into the world, at the halo of fuzzy blond curls that covered her head and the angelic face contorted with the effort to cry—a cry that sounded decidedly robust and healthy.

The newborn's eyelids flickered, then opened, and Mac found himself staring into a pair of startling blue eyes. An emotion he didn't recognize and refused to acknowledge clutched at his heart.

Sliding one hand under the baby's head for support, he handed the crying infant into Eve's outstretched arms.

''Congratulations! You have a beautiful daughter.''

Eve's mouth curved into a beaming smile, her eyes alight with joy as she gazed down at the baby in her arms.

''She is beautiful,'' Eve breathed, unable to believe she was actually holding her baby in her arms. She'd been looking forward to and dreading this moment, both at the same time. ''Absolutely beautiful,'' Eve repeated, awe and love threading through her voice.

''Just like her mother,'' Mac said.

Eve managed a feeble smile.

''You're exhausted,'' Mac continued. ''You need to rest.''

The baby's cries intensified.

"Maybe I should try feeding her," Eve said, anxiety lacing her tone.

Mac immediately took a step back. "I'll leave you to it." Gathering the soiled towels off the bed he quickly withdrew, closing the door behind him. He entered the bathroom and tossed the towels into the tub.

He turned on the tap and washed his hands. Being present during the labor and aiding in the birth of Eve's baby had left a deep and abiding impression.

For the first time in years his thoughts turned to his own mother, to the woman who'd abandoned him on the steps of a hospital only hours after giving birth.

Had she been alone during her labor? he wondered as he tugged a clean towel from the towel rack. Had she been scared out of her wits by the contractions?

He remembered a conversation he'd had with his adopted mother, Maggie, not long after she and Joe had signed the papers that made him an official member of their family.

He'd made a bitter comment about his mother dumping him, and, to his surprise, Maggie had risen to the other woman's defense. She'd suggested his mother might have been a frightened teenager who had chosen to give him up in the hope he would have a better life.

Surprised, and not a little angry at her compassionate tone, he'd swept aside Maggie's attempt to shed a different light on things. But witnessing what Eve had just gone through had given him a whole new perspective.

If Eve had been a frightened teen instead of a mature woman in her twenties, he doubted she would have been able to maintain her calm or stay in control.

She'd handled herself well. The speedy progression of her labor hadn't given either of them time to think about anything other than the baby's welfare.

He doubted he would ever forget the way she'd fought to maintain her focus while the contractions racked her body. Nor would he forget the way she'd calmly told him what to do during those last crucial stages of her labor.

Mac shivered. The chilly air penetrated his lightweight sweater, prompting him into action. He strode into the living room and moved to stand at the window.

Outside, large white flakes, swirling and spinning in the gusting wind, continued to fall from the dark sky. The possibility of returning to town had long since faded. They would be spending the night, and if the storm didn't let up, possibly longer.

Mac pulled the drapes closed, shutting out the

storm. He flicked the switch, smiling when the lights came on. At least they had electricity.

Needing some physical action, he turned his attention to lighting a fire. Heat was the first priority, food the next. He'd light a fire, then check the kitchen cupboards.

Using old newspapers and kindling from the basket on the hearth, he soon had a fire started. When he was satisfied the fire wouldn't go out, he replaced the fire guard and headed to the kitchen.

He explored the cupboards and found a stock of canned goods that included soups and salmon. "Thanks, big brother."

His stomach growled, and he acknowledged it had been a long time since lunch. Checking the freezer, he smiled when he saw a package of hamburger buns and two loaves of bread.

After locating the can opener, he used it to open a can of beef-and-vegetable soup. Deciding he should look in on Eve and the baby, he set the pot of soup on low heat, then made his way to the bedroom.

At the door he tapped lightly, then entered.

Eve lay against the pillows, eyes closed, the baby snuggled tightly in her arms. Mac moved closer, and Eve's eyes opened. She smiled up at him. "I can't seem to stay awake." Her voice was weighted with exhaustion. "I hate to ask. You've done so much

already. But could you look after the baby for me
while I have a nap?''

''Sure.'' Reaching down he gathered the sleeping
baby into his arms.

''Thank you...for everything,'' Eve murmured
before closing her eyes.

Mac glanced in silence at the sleeping infant. He
knew absolutely nothing about babies or how to take
care of them. What the hell was he supposed to do
now?

Chapter Five

Mac's gaze flicked back to Eve. Her breathing had deepened. She'd fallen asleep. He stood staring at her pale features, silently acknowledging she deserved a rest. She'd done one helluva job.

The baby whimpered, diverting his attention. He withdrew from Eve's room, carrying the baby to the living room.

Remembering the pot he'd left warming on the stove, he changed direction. To his relief the soup hadn't begun to boil. His hunger would have to wait. He turned off the element.

His thoughts drifted over the past few hours. Everything had happened so fast, from the moment he'd picked Eve up out of the snow, to the last contraction that had pushed the baby into the world.

He gazed down at the tiny bundle. How could he get anything done with a baby in his arms? He needed to find a safe place for her, a container of some kind, where she could stay warm and clean.

Estimating her weight to be between six and seven pounds, he thought a large roasting pan would work. He opened a few cupboards but found nothing he deemed suitable.

Then he remembered the picnic hamper he'd seen while searching the cupboards for food. After he managed, one-handedly, to haul it out, he set it on the kitchen table and studied it.

Two leather straps encircled the hamper making it look like an old-fashioned suitcase. Mac unbuckled the straps and flipped open the lid. Packed neatly inside he found everything essential for a picnic.

He only needed the top half. With a knife he cut through the thick leather straps. His left arm ached with the weight of the baby, and he could feel tiny beads of perspiration forming on his brow as he worked.

When the hamper lid fell to the floor with a loud thump, Mac glanced at the baby, sure the noise would waken her. To his relief she slept on. Picking up the lid, he carried it through to where the fire burned bright and the room was appreciably warmer.

He set the lid on the oval rug, a safe distance from the fire, and gingerly lowered the baby into it. The towel wrapped around the baby caught on the edge of the hamper and fell open to reveal two plump legs.

Mac gazed at the exposed limbs and tiny feet, awed by both the size and the delicate detail. A smile tugged at his mouth as he cupped his hand around one baby foot, but his smile changed to a frown when he discovered her toes were cold.

He covered her legs, but not before realizing the towel was damp. He sat back on his heels, his thoughts racing. From his experience rescuing lost or stranded skiers in the freezing temperatures of the Alps, he knew the dangers wet clothes presented. Common sense told him leaving a baby, especially a newborn, wrapped in a damp towel constituted a definite risk.

The answer was simple. She needed a diaper or something that would work just as well. A towel would do it. He headed for the cupboard in the hall, but he'd only taken a few steps when the baby started to cry.

Mac knelt down again, his heart thundering. Not for the first time he wished himself a thousand miles away. Had the baby started crying because of hunger or because she was cold and wet? What about all three? Should he pick her up?

Indecision swamped him. He'd always been a take-charge kind of guy, but for the first time in his adult life he didn't have the foggiest notion what to do.

The cries grew louder and more insistent. Mac lifted the baby into his arms, instantly noticing that the towel felt both warm and wetter. That had to be the problem.

He held her against his neck, careful to support her head, as well as give her enough room to breathe. He rocked back and forth, the way he'd seen women do when holding a fussy child, and to his surprise and relief her cries diminished.

Reluctant to set her down, he carried her into the hall. From the closet he withdrew several large towels, tucking them under his free arm. Then he noticed a stack of smaller hand towels, almost the right size to encompass a baby's bottom.

Grabbing a handful, he returned to the living room. With clumsy hands he struggled to discard the wet towel. Naked and wriggling, the baby let out a cry of protest.

By the time he placed her onto the dry towel he'd spread out in the basket, sweat had begun to trickle down his back.

Mac sat back on his haunches and surveyed the situation. Impossible as it seemed, the baby had stopped crying. Should he even bother with a diaper? He didn't much relish the task. Still, the diaper would create a degree of warmth, and the outer towel would stay dry longer.

Folding one of the hand towels in two, he tucked it under her tiny bottom and started to wrap the makeshift diaper around each leg. He soon realized he had no means of securing the ends. Knowing she would be safe and warm in the hamper on the floor, he hurried into the kitchen in search of a safety pin, tape, anything.

Desperate, he searched the toolbox by the back door and found a roll of duct tape. Clutching his prize, he returned to the living room and knelt down beside the hamper. To his surprise the baby's eyes were open.

Mac stopped to study the angelic face. A pair of bright-blue eyes framed by long curling lashes gazed up at him. Her nose was the size of a button, and her mouth looked like a miniature bow.

He'd never been this up close and personal with a baby before. He'd made it a policy never to let himself become too involved in other people's lives. Involvement led to heartache, a lesson he'd learned the hard way.

A small arm poked its way free of the towel. Her tiny fingers were curled into a fist, as if she'd punched her way out. Captivated, Mac touched the baby's hand with his index finger. At the contact the tiny fist unfurled like the petals of a flower, to reveal the minuscule creases and lines of her palm. Mesmerized, he traced her lifeline with his nail, then gasped in astonishment when she captured his finger in a grip that startled him with its strength.

For a second it felt as if his heart was being

squeezed in a vise. The muscles in his chest tight-ened, and an emotion he couldn't begin to describe blossomed inside him. When her tiny hand surren-dered its hold, Mac couldn't quite fathom the feeling of disappointment that stabbed at him. With a shake of his head he refocused on the task of fastening the makeshift diaper.

After securing the diaper in place and tucking the towel around her once more, Mac sat back to admire his work. Rising, he stretched his cramped legs. The windowpanes rattled as a gust of wind hit the cabin. At the sudden noise the baby started to cry.

Mac glanced at his watch. It didn't seem possible that only an hour had passed. The baby's cries in-tensified. Crouching down, he gathered her into his arms and headed to the bedroom.

Eve greeted him with a sleepy smile and eased herself into a sitting position. "Sounds like she's got a strong pair of lungs," she said, above the baby's urgent cries.

"That's an understatement."

"I'll try feeding her again. Maybe that will soothe her."

"Good idea," Mac said, already retreating. He stopped in the doorway and turned. "I'm heating a can of soup. Would you like a bowl when you're done?"

"Sounds wonderful. Thank you."

Alone with her daughter, Eve gazed down at the

baby, her tiny face red from exertion, her mouth opening and closing like a baby bird in search of food.

"Shh. Don't cry, my love." She unbuttoned her top. But it was several frustrating, noisy minutes later before Eve succeeded in coaxing the baby to take her nipple.

The baby's cries stopped abruptly, and Eve let out a sigh as she relaxed against the pillows. The towel wrapped around the baby had come undone giving Eve a bird's-eye view of the duct tape holding together a makeshift diaper. Eve laughed softly. Mac was nothing if not resourceful.

As the baby suckled, Eve found her thoughts drifting back to those intense moments leading up to the birth. While she sensed Mac hadn't been comfortable throughout her labor, he'd stayed with her.

She wasn't sure when it had happened, but at some point during the birth she'd put her trust in him, believing he would take care of her and the baby, that he wouldn't let her down. Together they'd participated in a miracle, sharing the unforgettable intimacy of the birth of a baby. She doubted she'd ever forget this day, or how grateful she'd been for his help and stoic presence.

Her body ached all over, but the nap had restored some of her strength. She gazed in wonder at the miracle in her arms, taking in every minute, perfect detail. She still couldn't believe that this beautiful baby was her daughter, her very own child, her family—all the family she might ever have.

She'd always dreamed of having a family of her own, and for a while had harbored the hope that Larry would be the man she'd spend the rest of her life with, have babies with. His betrayal had shocked and hurt her. She'd prided herself on being a good judge of character. The discovery of how easily she'd been duped, how readily she'd fallen for his charms and how willing she'd been to ignore her inner voice, had shaken her.

That he'd run off with her life's savings had been bad enough, but by not protecting herself from pregnancy, she knew she'd behaved irresponsibly. She had only herself to blame. She'd been far too eager to believe his promises and too blind to see that his charm was nothing but a facade.

At first the prospect of becoming a single parent had frightened and overwhelmed her. David's friendship and support had helped her come to terms with her predicament and allowed her to plan a future for herself and her baby.

She'd vowed to raise her child in a loving, caring atmosphere. And when her daughter started asking questions about her father, she wouldn't lie. She would say that she'd made a bad choice, that her father hadn't been an honorable man, then she would tell her daughter about another man, the one who'd helped deliver her safely into the world and about his brother, David.

Eve sighed. How she wished David could see the baby, hold this beautiful, precious gift. She'd asked David if he would be the baby's godfather, an honor he'd happily accepted.

A light tap on the bedroom door had her blinking back tears. She glanced up to see Mac with a tray in his hands. His gaze dropped to the baby suckling at her breast, lingering there for several heartbeats.

When his gaze lifted to meet hers, Eve caught the flicker of heat that flashed in his gray eyes, before a shutter came crashing down. "I'm sorry," Mac said. "I should have waited. Give me a shout when you're ready," he added before withdrawing.

Eve continued to stare at the spot where Mac had been standing. What had passed between them during those brief seconds had been sexual awareness. She should be angry that he would think of her in that way, instead she'd felt an answering quiver of response. How could she, after having given birth only a few hours before, feel such a sharp tug of attraction? Her hormones were obviously to blame.

Her daughter stirred, distracting her. As Eve lifted the baby, her glance strayed to the window and the snow continuing to fall. Eve shivered, noticing now that the temperature in the room had dropped several degrees. She wrapped the towel tightly around the baby and slid to the edge of the bed. Placing the baby in the center of the bed, she stood up and shuffled to the closet in search of something warm to wear.

With some relief she spotted a thick terry cloth bathrobe hanging behind the closet door. Slipping it on, she felt glad of its weight and warmth. She rolled up the sleeves a little and tied the belt loosely around her waist. After checking to make sure the baby hadn't stirred, she made her way to the bathroom across the hall.

While she would have loved to fill the bathtub and soak for an hour, she made do with a washcloth and soap. Wrapped in the terry robe once more, she returned to the bedroom and gathering the sleeping baby in her arms padded to the living room.

"I could use that soup right about now," Eve said.

Mac rose from the recliner. "I would have brought it to you."

"Thanks, but it's getting quite cold in the bedroom, and I could smell the fire."

"Is she asleep?" he asked.

"Yes."

"I made a bed for her." Mac pointed to the hamper on the rug. "It's the top half of an old picnic hamper," he added in response to her frown.

"How ingenious," she said. "And the perfect size. Unfortunately, I don't think I can bend down that far. Would you mind?"

"No problem." As Mac took the sleeping baby from her arms, his hands brushed hers, and a jolt of sensation arced through her. Their glances collided, and Eve glimpsed raw pain in the depths of his gray eyes.

The baby let out a plaintive cry, fracturing the moment. Mac's expression changed to one of concern as his gaze shifted to the baby.

"It's okay little one. Hush." Mac spoke softly, his words like a soothing caress, and Eve watched, marveling at the tenderness in his voice.

Mac smiled with relief when the baby grew silent once more. He crouched to place her in the hamper bed. "She'll be safe and warm there."

"You handle her well."

Mac threw her a startled glance. "I do?" he asked, surprised.

Eve smiled and nodded. "Some men tend to shy away from babies, especially newborns. I don't think David could have done what you did. Helped at the birth, I mean. You were so confident and calm, that alone helped keep me focused. You were wonderful."

Mac shifted uncomfortably. "How about that bowl of soup and a sandwich?" he asked, his tone abrupt. As he moved away, Eve noted the hint of color staining his cheeks.

"Lead me to it," she replied.

"No! Stay here where it's warm. I'll bring a tray through."

Before she could respond, he strode off.

Eve lowered herself onto the sofa, enjoying the warmth generated by the fire. Her thoughts turned to Mac. If the faint blush she'd just witnessed was anything to go by, he'd seemed both surprised and embarrassed by her compliment.

She shook her head. He was a complex man. A man she'd made up her mind to dislike, even before she'd set eyes on him. And thanks to her attitude they hadn't exactly gotten off on the right foot. But he'd come through in the crunch. Without him she would never have been able to endure her labor or the baby's birth. He'd been her rock, her salvation.

She glanced at the baby asleep in the bed Mac had fashioned. A smile tugged at her mouth when she remembered the makeshift diaper.

"Eve?" Her name on his lips startled her. She hadn't heard him approach.

"Thanks." She took the tray from him, making sure their hands didn't touch. "I seem to be saying 'thank you' a lot. I don't know what I would have done if you hadn't been here."

"You'd be where you should be, in the hospital under the care of nurses and doctors," he replied dryly.

Eve heard the self-reproach in his voice. "How were you supposed to know I'd go into early labor?'' she countered. ''Besides, I think we coped rather well, and the end result made it all worthwhile, don't you agree?'' She glanced down at the baby in the hamper at her feet.

''I'd still feel better if we had a doctor or nurse here to check both you and the baby.''

''We're fine,'' she said with more confidence than she felt. ''Women have babies at home all the time and in conditions far more rustic than this,'' she added, wanting to assure him she had no hard feelings.

She set the tray on her knees, then laughed. ''Do you know, I haven't been able to hold anything on my lap for months,'' she explained, before bringing the spoon to her lips.

''Did you, by any chance, tell anyone at the inn where we were headed?'' Mac asked, changing the subject.

Eve lowered the spoon and frowned. ''I said I'd be gone the rest of the day, but I didn't mention where we were going. I assumed we'd be back in a couple of hours.''

Mac made no reply. He crouched to take a log from the wood bin on the hearth. Pulling aside the fireguard, he placed the log on the flames.

''Surely we'll be able to leave in the morning.''

Mac settled in the recliner once more. ''Time will tell, but the way the snow's been coming down, I wouldn't bet on it.''

Chapter Six

Eve pondered Mac's words for a long moment. She supposed she was naive in assuming the snow would stop during the night, allowing them to make the return journey to Cypress Crossing in the morning. She could hear the wind howling outside and tried to ignore the anxiety threading through her at the realization that they were indeed stranded.

"How long do you think we'll have to stay?" she asked, glancing with some concern at the baby asleep in the lid of the hamper, silently acknowledging that she, too, would feel happier once they were both checked over by a doctor.

"There's no telling what the roads will be like come morning," Mac said. "You know this area better than I do. Judging by the conditions on the drive here, I'd say they're cleared on a regular basis. Am I right?''

"The main roads are the first priority, of course,'' Eve answered. "This route is a bit off the beaten track, but it is cleared eventually.'' She sighed. "I wish I'd thought to grab David's cell phone.''

"I thought you said it didn't work in this area, anyway,'' Mac commented.

"That's true, but we could have tried…''

"Let's see how things look in the morning,'' Mac said. "David's truck is a four-wheel drive. It can handle poor conditions better than most vehicles. I'll dig it out, and we could try getting back to the main road. In the meantime we're warm and dry.''

"Where will you sleep?'' Eve asked.

"Right here.'' Mac patted the reclining chair. "I plan to keep the fire burning all night, and that firewood stacked outside should last a few days.''

"You think we'll be here that long?'' Worry laced her voice.

"It's a possibility. Did David cut the wood himself?'' Mac asked, lowering himself into the chair.

"I'm not sure.'' He'd changed the subject, no doubt in an attempt to distract her.

"In any case, I'd much rather be here than wandering around a mountainside in freezing temperatures looking for lost skiers.''

"Do you get called out on rescue missions often?'' Eve asked, puzzled by the hollow note in his voice.

He sighed. ''Too often.''

''You didn't answer my question earlier about avalanches,'' she said, recalling his unusual reaction. ''Are they very common?''

She watched his mouth tighten seconds before he stood up and strode to the window, tension in every line of his body.

''I didn't mean to upset you. I'm sorry. There've been a few avalanches lately in this ski area. Thankfully, no one's been hurt.''

Mac remained silent, his thoughts shifting to that night not so long ago when he'd experienced firsthand the incredible power behind an avalanche.

''Avalanches aren't all that common,'' he said at last, keeping his tone even. ''But the threat is constant and not to be ignored.''

''I imagine it would be horrifying to be caught in one,'' she said with a shiver.

At her comment a shudder rolled through him. He spun away from the window and crossed to the fireplace.

''Horrifying doesn't begin to describe it.'' Mac stared into the flames. Other than giving a report to the police investigating the deaths of the two English students and his colleague, he hadn't spoken to anyone about his ordeal, not even the trauma counselor who'd paid him a visit in the hospital.

"Are you talking from personal experience?" Eve asked. He found the quiet sympathy in her voice disconcerting. His vision blurred, and pain seared his heart as the memory of that night, of being hurled down the mountain, washed over him once more. Three lives had been lost on that mountain. He'd come close to being the fourth.

"Mac? Are you all right?" The genuine concern in Eve's voice brought a lump of emotion to his throat, making it impossible for him to respond. Dropping into the nearby recliner, he leaned forward to rest his elbows on his knees, keeping his gaze averted from hers.

"I'm right, aren't I?" Eve said, certainty and compassion in her voice. "You and your team were out on a rescue mission, that's why you didn't return my call, and why you weren't able to get here in time for David's funeral."

Her hand came out to cover his in a gesture that stole his breath and brought his heart to a shuddering halt before it raced off once more.

Mac couldn't recall the last time anyone had ever touched him to offer comfort. Beneath her fingers he could feel her warmth seeping into him, spreading through him like a healing balm, awakening an emotion he didn't want to feel.

He leaned back in the chair, breaking the contact. "Yes, we were out on a rescue mission," he acknowledged in a hoarse whisper. "Not that it matters now."

"Of course it matters," Eve said earnestly. "If I'd known, I would have delayed the funeral service until you could get here. Why didn't you call once you returned from the rescue mission?"

"I couldn't."

"You couldn't? I don't understand." She frowned.

"There's no point—"

"Please," Eve cut in. "Tell me what happened."

Mac met her gaze. Her compassion and understanding began to dispel the chill that had settled around his heart.

"The gondolas and ski lifts were closing for the day when we got the call," he began, surprised at how easily the words came.

"Four skiers from a group of teenage students on a pre-Christmas trip from England had been reported missing. Several teams were assembled, and we headed to the area where the four had last been seen. The teams split up to do a sweep, and an hour later we found tracks leading to an area of the mountain that's off-limits."

"Did you find them?"

"We found them." Anger and sorrow edged his tone. "They were cold and frightened and close to panic. They'd been walking around in circles until one of them decided they should stay put and wait to be rescued.''

''I bet they were glad to see you.''

Mac nodded. ''I wanted to read them the riot act for skiing out of bounds, but I figured they'd already learned a valuable lesson. Unfortunately, the night wasn't quite over—'' He broke off. Lowering his head, he speared both hands through his thick dark hair, despair in every gesture. ''The avalanche…''

Eve reached out and touched his arm. She could feel the tension vibrating through him. He raised his head and met her gaze once more.

''Go on,'' she coaxed.

''I'd just finished radioing the command post telling them we'd located the group when we all heard the thunderous roar.'' He said nothing for a moment as if listening to the sound again. ''We didn't have time to think or react,'' he went on in a whisper. ''The next thing I remember is being swept down the mountainside by the snow and fighting to stay on top.''

''Oh, Mac! How awful! But you survived, you're here.'' She squeezed his arm.

''Thanks to the intensive training we do, I made it,'' he replied, a mixture of guilt and sadness in his voice.

''What about the students and the rest of your team?'' Eve asked, knowing from the grim expression on Mac's face there was no happy ending.

Mac pulled away to massage the back of his neck. "Two students and one member of my team died in the avalanche."

"I'm so sorry."

"The fact that I'd radioed our position helped the other teams locate us," Mac went on. "But not soon enough."

"Were you hurt?" she asked, concern in her voice now.

"I hit my head on something on my way down," he said. "I don't remember much until I woke up in the hospital."

"No broken bones?"

He shook his head. "A few bumps and bruises but nothing broken. The doctors said I'd suffered a concussion, and they insisted on keeping me in for observation."

"How long were you kept in the hospital?"

"Four days."

"That long?" she asked, thinking the concussion he'd suffered had to have been severe.

"I didn't get your message until I returned home," Mac continued.

Shock ricocheted through her. "So you knew nothing about David's death until you got home from the hospital?"

"That's right."

"Mac, I'm so sorry. That explains why you didn't return my call. When I didn't hear a word from you

I thought—'' Eve broke off, realizing that she'd misjudged him, badly. From his obvious distress she could see he had cared about David a great deal, and learning about his brother's death on top of the horror of the avalanche had to have been devastating.

''I couldn't quite take it in at first,'' Mac said, a heaviness in his voice.

''And no wonder,'' Eve countered, feeling ashamed. ''I owe you an apology. I should have tried harder to contact you.''

A smile flitted across his features. ''I doubt you'd have been able to track me down at the hospital.''

''I couldn't understand why I hadn't heard from you, especially when David had always spoken so highly of you,'' she went on.

Mac's gaze darted to meet hers, sadness and regret shimmering in the gray eyes. ''He did?''

''He was proud of you, of how well you'd done for yourself in Switzerland. He enjoyed his visits with you every summer, but I think he wished you'd come to Cypress Crossing. Why didn't you?'' she asked.

Her question hung in the air between them. The only sound was the wood crackling in the hearth and the wind howling outside. The silence was broken by the baby's cry, and Eve struggled to pick her up.

''I'll get her.'' Mac leaned over and lifted the baby from the makeshift bed. As he handed the tiny bundle to Eve, his hand brushed her breast, leaving a tingle in its wake.

Eve ignored her body's response to his touch, focusing her attention on her daughter. "She's wet. I'd better change her."

"There's a couple of small towels under the tray beside you." Mac said, reaching to remove the tray. "Oh, and you'll need this." He held out the roll of duct tape.

"Thanks."

"Have you decided on a name for the baby?"

Eve smiled down at her daughter. During her pregnancy, she'd read a number of baby books in search of a name she liked, but hadn't been able to decide on one. Now that the baby had arrived, now that she'd seen her daughter, she knew a name that would fit perfectly.

"I'm going to call her Hope."

Hope. The name suited the baby, Mac thought a few minutes later as he stood in the kitchen washing dishes. Not for the first time he found himself wondering about the baby's father.

After thinking things over, he felt sure Eve had told him the truth. David wasn't Hope's father. It would have been to her advantage to make the claim, especially since the baby would have been the rightful heir to David's estate.

But if not David, then who? Had the guy run off

when she'd told him she was pregnant? Had Eve named the baby Hope because she still loved the baby's father and hoped to be reunited with him? This last thought disturbed him more than he cared to admit.

His experience with the baby had made him realize that fathering a child and being a father were dramatically different. Until now he'd had no idea the level of responsibility and commitment a baby required. Eve's comment that he seemed at ease with the baby had surprised and pleased him. But he couldn't see himself as a father. He knew nothing of parenting.

As he rinsed the soup bowls he found his thoughts turning to Eve. It had come as something of a surprise to find himself recounting the story of what happened up on the mountain. He'd never been one to unburden himself to anyone and certainly not to a woman he barely knew.

She'd listened without censure, without judgment, and when she'd reached out to him, the touch of her hand had somehow soothed his aching heart.

He'd never met a woman like her. And while he'd been known to enjoy a woman's company from time to time, he'd made it a rule to never let his emotions become involved, to keep a firm hold on his heart.

Emotional involvement ultimately led to pain and heartache. It was a lesson he'd learned well during his childhood. Everyone who'd ever meant anything to him—the woman who'd given him life, Maggie and Joe, and now his brother, David—had all been taken from him.

Even Genevieve, the sweet young girl he'd fallen in love with in Rome during his travels, hadn't found him lovable enough to want to stick around. After what had been an idyllic two months together, Genevieve had slipped away one night while he slept, leaving him devastated and alone. It's what had cemented his decision to keep people at a distance, to avoid emotional entanglements of any kind.

By the time he'd settled in the small hillside town in the Swiss Alps, he'd become adept at sidestepping involvements, at politely turning down invitations, at keeping his private life private.

He'd grown accustomed to spending time alone, telling himself he liked it that way, that he preferred the peace and quiet his lifestyle afforded. While he did have a number of friends, several of whom worked in the hotel industry and others he'd met as a result of his volunteer work with the rescue team, he'd managed to maintain a distance.

The fact that David had bothered to track him down had surprised him, and at first he hadn't been eager to reestablish a relationship with his brother, even though David's presence reminded him of happier times. David had refused to play by the rules, breaking down Mac's defenses and defying all his attempts to keep David at arm's length. Mac had to admit that his brother's friendship had come to mean more to him than he'd ever been able to say. David's death left an empty void, deeper and colder and lonelier than any before.

Mac closed his eyes against the wave of sorrow washing over him. His head began to throb and he could feel perspiration breaking out on his forehead, a symptom of the concussion he'd suffered. The medication he'd been prescribed for just such an occurrence was in his bag back at the condo.

"Damn it! Not now!" he muttered under his breath. He'd planned to haul in wood from the pile outside, enough to keep the fire going throughout the night. But now he gripped the edge of the sink, fighting back the nausea and dizziness assailing him.

Chapter Seven

"Mac? Are you all right?" Eve's voice seemed to come from somewhere far away. "Here, you'd better sit down."

He heard the sound of a chair scraping against the wooden floor and lowered himself into it with a grateful sigh even as he continued to fight the dizziness. Moments later he felt the soothing comfort of a cool, wet cloth being pressed against his forehead.

"Thanks. I'll be fine." He raised his hand to the wet cloth, trapping Eve's fingers beneath his own for a brief moment.

"What happened?" she asked.

"I felt dizzy, that's all," he told her, struggling to regain his composure.

"You mentioned medication last night," Eve said. "Are you taking something?"

Mac nodded. "Pills that are supposed to relieve the symptoms."

"How often do you take them?"

"When I feel a headache coming on," he replied. "But they don't help much."

"Maybe you should lie down and rest for a while," Eve suggested.

He lowered the cloth and met her worried gaze. "I will, right after I bring in enough firewood to last us the night." He started to get up.

Eve placed a restraining hand on his shoulder. "Stay where you are for a few more minutes," she ordered in a voice that brooked no argument. "If you go outside in these freezing temperatures and start hauling in firewood, you're liable to collapse."

Mac met her gaze, seeing the concern and the fear lurking just below the surface. For a mind-blowing second the desire to pull her into his arms and tell her everything would be all right was almost more than he could resist.

They stared at each other for what seemed like an eternity. Eve broke away first, turning to the sink. "I came for a glass of water. Would you like one?" she asked over her shoulder.

"Yes, thanks." Mac stood up, relieved to discover that his nausea had subsided and the throbbing in his head had lessened to a dull ache.

"Are you sure you're okay?" she asked as she handed him the water.

"I'm fine." He managed a weak smile of reassurance before taking a sip.

"I'd better check on the baby." She started to leave, then stopped. She faced him once more. "We need to figure out sleeping arrangements. The bedroom is too cold. I think we should sleep together in the living room."

Eve saw a glint of amusement dance in the depths of his gray eyes and felt her face grow warm as she realized what she'd said.

"I mean...it's much warmer by the fire," she hurried to explain. "The sofa is a pullout so we can sleep together—" She broke off.

Mac's features creased into a smile. "What you're trying to say is that you and Hope will sleep on the sofa bed while I take the reclining chair."

"Yes," Eve agreed with relief, ignoring the quicksilver shiver that chased through her in response to his smile.

"I'll get the blankets from the bedroom, you'll need those," Mac said as he headed in that direction.

Eve returned to the living room and sat down on the sofa. Her thoughts turned to Mac and how pale he'd looked. Guilt at having misjudged him washed over her again. She prayed the storm would blow itself out and they would be able to leave in the morning.

Her gaze shifted to her baby—perfect from the top of her blond hair to her ten chubby toes. Eve had never experienced this depth of feeling for anyone before. It was frightening and wonderful at the same time.

She had a daughter. They were a family. And while her dreams of becoming a parent had always included a husband, a man she loved with all her heart, after her experience with Larry she doubted she would ever be able to trust another man. Besides, her daughter's welfare was Eve's first priority and more important than any man.

"Here are the blankets from the bed," Mac said when he appeared a few minutes later with an armful of bedding. "I found this sleeping bag in the bedroom closet. I'll use it."

Eve stood up. "We might as well pull the bed out now."

"I'll get it." Mac dropped the blankets and sleeping bag on the reclining chair and proceeded to remove the cushions from the sofa. Once he'd pulled the bed out, he reached for the blankets. Eve stepped to the opposite side and, working together, they made up the bed.

"I forgot pillows," Mac said, and strode down the hall, returning a few moments later with three pillows.

"Could you lift the baby's basket onto the bed for me?" Eve asked.

Mac tossed the pillows aside and bent to lift the basket with the sleeping baby onto the bed. "There you go."

"Thanks. Do you know what time it is?" Eve asked, having totally lost track of how long they'd been at the cabin.

Mac glanced at his watch. "It's almost eight," he said. "I'd better bring the wood in before we settle for the night."

"Are you sure you're—" Eve began.

"I'm fine," Mac said. "Maybe you could man the door for me, that way we can limit how much cold air gets in."

"Okay." Eve came around the sofa bed and crossed to the cabin door. For the next ten minutes they worked together.

"That should do it," Mac said on the sixth load.

Eve closed the door and followed him to the fire. Chilled, she sat on the corner of the sofa bed nearest the fire, huddled inside the housecoat.

"What made you decide to settle in Switzerland?" she asked as Mac brushed bits of bark off the front of his sweater.

"I'd grown weary of moving from place to place," he said, readjusting the firescreen.

"How long had you been on the road?" Eve asked.

"More than a year."

"Why didn't you ever come to Cypress Crossing?" she asked, and saw him stiffen at her question.

After a lengthy pause he said, "It never seemed to work out."

"That's a pretty pathetic excuse," Eve commented as he moved to unzip the sleeping bag. "David was your only relative, and for the six years I knew him, he spent several weeks every summer visiting you in Switzerland."

Mac's gaze met hers, and she saw irritation and regret in his eyes.

"I'm sorry," she said. "It's really none of my business."

"You're right, it is none of your business," Mac acknowledged, an edge to his tone. He turned away and continued to arrange the sleeping bag on the reclining chair. "What about you?" he asked. "Do you have family you keep in touch with?"

"No, I don't have a family," she replied in an even tone.

"None here in Cypress Crossing, you mean."

"None, anywhere," she replied, "except for Hope, of course," she added with a smile at her sleeping daughter.

"No parents, brothers or sisters?" he asked as he sat down on the reclining chair.

"My parents died six years ago before I moved

to Cypress Crossing. My father had a heart attack shortly after he retired, and my mother died a few months later of a broken heart.''

"I'm sorry," he said, his tone sincere.

Eve nodded in acknowledgment. "As for brothers and sisters, I don't have any. My parents were in their mid-forties when I came along. You could say I was an unwelcome surprise," she told him, sadness in her voice.

"They didn't want you?" Surprise echoed through his words.

She smiled. "Let's just say they weren't cut out to be parents. They knew nothing about raising a child, or about how to take care of a baby. They were both very involved with their careers."

"What did they do?" Mac asked.

"My father taught mathematics at the University of British Columbia in Vancouver, and my mother taught English there, too. That's where they met. Apparently, they'd agreed when they got married they weren't going to have children. My arrival posed something of a problem."

"And how did they solve...the problem?" Mac asked.

"From as far back as I can remember, to the time I reached the age of twelve, I had a stream of nannies and baby-sitters," she told him. Her caregivers had changed so often during her early years that she'd never become attached to any of them.

At the age of four she'd been allowed to join her parents occasionally for their evening meal, a concession that hadn't always been a pleasant experience. She'd much preferred her own company or the company of the current nanny.

"And after that?" Mac prompted.

"I learned to look after myself," Eve replied with a hint of pride. "What about you?" she asked, turning the tables. "David told me his parents adopted you when you were a teen."

"That's right." Mac shifted restlessly.

"They must have been special people to take on a teenage boy," she went on, hoping Mac would elaborate.

The silence stretched, and Eve glanced at Mac, noticing that his eyes were closed. Was he ignoring her? Or had he fallen asleep?

Her heart skipped a beat as she recalled how ill he'd looked when she'd walked into the kitchen and found him bent over the sink. Panic gripped her. Had his headache returned? Maybe he'd lost consciousness? She started to rise....

"The Kingstons were very special people." Mac's voice vibrated with pain and sorrow.

"You still miss them," Eve stated simply, surprised by the revelation. Since his arrival in Cypress Crossing he'd seemed both cold and arrogant. But throughout their ordeal she'd seen another side to this man, a softer side, a caring side.

She looked at him again, but his eyes remained closed. Only the pulse throbbing at his jaw revealed emotions he seemed determined to hold in check.

"What about your parents? Why did they put you up for adoption in the first place?" she asked, her curiosity roused.

This time Eve was sure Mac had fallen asleep. The silence stretched far longer than before. Beside her Hope started to whimper.

"I never knew my parents." Mac's deep, resonant voice, devoid of any emotion, startled Eve. "They didn't want me, at least my mother didn't," he amended. "But she didn't hire a nanny or a babysitter, she left me on the steps of a hospital a few hours after I was born."

Stunned, Eve couldn't think of a thing to say. Hope's cries grew louder, erupting into a full-fledged wail.

Distracted, Eve reached into the basket to lift her daughter into her arms. As she cooed soft words of comfort, of love, her thoughts turned to another baby, a baby almost the same age as Hope, a baby abandoned by his mother.

She glanced toward Mac, hoping he would continue his story and tell her more about his childhood, but he'd turned his back to her, a strong indication that the conversation was over.

For the remainder of the night, whenever the baby slept Eve caught a few hours of shut-eye. Several times during those waking moments she heard the reclining chair creak as Mac rose to tend the fire.

Outside, the storm gave no sign of abating. The wind continued to howl, and when she ventured from the warmth of the sofa bed to visit the bathroom, she hadn't been surprised to see snow still falling.

Two hours later a noise woke her. A moan or a whimper, she wasn't quite sure. At first she thought Hope had awakened, but a quick check confirmed the baby slept on.

The sound came again. Louder this time.

Eve glanced at Mac stretched out in the reclining chair. Another moan escaped, and his head began to move from side to side in obvious agitation.

Eve rose and moved to stand by the chair, trying to decide if she should awaken him. She let her gaze linger on his handsome face. She watched as his expression relaxed, and, as she studied him, she could easily imagine what he'd looked like as a young child.

Those thick, dark curls and long, black eyelashes would have been evident as a baby. And how could anyone forget the grayest eyes she'd ever seen? Eyes that at times were as cold and icy as a shower of sleet, and at other times sparkling like diamonds in the sun.

She found herself wondering what dire circum-

The Silhouette Reader Service™ — Here's how it works:

Accepting your 2 free books and gift places you under no obligation to buy anything. You may keep the books and gift and return the shipping statement marked "cancel." If you do not cancel, about a month later we'll send you 6 additional novels and bill you just $3.34 each in the U.S., or $3.80 each in Canada, plus 25¢ shipping & handling per book and applicable taxes if any.* That's the complete price and — compared to cover prices of $3.99 each in the U.S. and $4.50 each in Canada — it's quite a bargain! You may cancel at any time, but if you choose to continue, every month we'll send you 6 more books, which you may either purchase at the discount price or return to us and cancel your subscription.

*Terms and prices subject to change without notice. Sales tax applicable in N.Y. Canadian residents will be charged applicable provincial taxes and GST.

GET FREE BOOKS and a FREE GIFT WHEN YOU PLAY THE...

Just scratch off the silver box with a coin. Then check below to see the gifts you get!

SLOT MACHINE GAME!

YES! I have scratched off the silver box. Please send me the 2 free Silhouette Romance® books and gift for which I qualify. I understand I am under no obligation to purchase any books, as explained on the back of this card.

315 SDL DQLM

215 SDL DRNJ
(S-R-11/02)

| FIRST NAME | LAST NAME |

| ADDRESS |

| APT.# | CITY |

| STATE/PROV. | ZIP/POSTAL CODE |

7 7 7   Worth TWO FREE BOOKS plus a BONUS Mystery Gift!

🍒 🍒 🍒   Worth TWO FREE BOOKS!

♣ ♣ ♣   Worth ONE FREE BOOK!

🔔 🔔 🍒   TRY AGAIN!

Visit us online at www.eHarlequin.com

DETACH AND MAIL CARD TODAY!

stances had led his mother to abandon him. No doubt after being found outside the hospital, he'd spent his first few months in foster care before being put up for adoption. But, according to what David had told her, the Kingstons hadn't adopted Mac until he was a teenager. Where, then, had Mac spent the first twelve years of his life? In foster care?

"No!" The cry came from Mac, making her gasp in surprise. He sat bolt-upright, his eyes wide, an expression of dismay on his face.

Eve put her hand on his shoulder. "Mac, it's all right, you're safe." She kept her tone even, while her heart beat a rapid tattoo against her ribs.

Mac blinked several times, then released his breath in a long sigh.

"Sorry. I hope I didn't frighten you," he said as he speared a hand through his hair.

"Must have been some nightmare," Eve said. "Do you remember any of it?"

He met her gaze, then shook his head. "No, nothing," he said, before looking away. "Did you get any sleep?" he asked as he pushed the sleeping bag aside.

"A little," she replied as she retreated to the sofa.

"Has it stopped snowing?" He stood and moving to the window, reached for the drapes.

"Not since the last time I looked out, a couple of hours ago," she said.

He stopped and threw her a glance over his shoulder. "It'll be bright out there. Will it waken the baby if I open these?" he asked.

"She's not facing the window," Eve replied, touched by his concern. Mac tugged the drapes open. He'd been right, the brightness was almost blinding.

"Wow!" Raising her hand, she shielded her eyes until she'd grown accustomed to the glare. She joined him at the window and gazed in awe at the pristine whiteness spreading as far as the eye could see.

"Quite the picture," Mac said. "At least it's stopped snowing. The storm must have blown itself out. I'd say a couple of feet and more has fallen since we got here yesterday."

"The truck's buried in a snowdrift." Eve pointed to the mound of snow covering the vehicle.

"Do you think the road crew will make it this far today?" he asked.

"I don't know," she replied, trying to keep the anxiety out of her voice. "I imagine if the general area has been hit this hard, the snow-clearing crew will have their hands full."

"I'll see if I can find a snow shovel to dig the truck out," Mac said. "If I can get the truck to the main road maybe we'll come upon one of the crews."

Eve sent up a silent prayer that they would make it out. Her concern wasn't for herself but for her baby. While Hope seemed healthy and appeared to be getting some sustenance, Eve's milk hadn't come in yet.

The literature she'd read on the subject had stated that a mother's milk didn't come in until the second or third day after the birth. She'd also learned from her perusal of the books that if a new mother was under any kind of stress, her chances of being able to breast-feed diminished considerably.

Worrying wouldn't help matters. She needed to focus on the positives. They had shelter. They were warm and dry. They had food. Hope was a strong, healthy baby and so far had come through the ordeal unscathed.

The storm appeared to be over. And she knew Mac would do everything in his power to get them out. He'd done an admirable job of looking after them so far. She had to put her trust in him, have faith he would be able to dig out the truck and drive them to safety.

"If I'm going to try to get us out of here today, I'd better get started," Mac said.

Chapter Eight

Mac spent the better part of the morning digging a path to and around the truck. But when he climbed in and turned the key, the engine coughed, spluttered, then died.

Eve spent the morning taking care of the baby. She'd boiled water and given Hope a sponge bath in front of the fire. After the bath she'd fed the baby, put her down for a nap, added more logs to the fire, then checked the kitchen cupboards in order to determine the extent of their food supplies.

Around one o'clock she'd called Mac for lunch.

"There's something wrong with the truck. It won't start," he told her as he sat down to eat.

"Can you fix it?" she asked.

"If I knew what the problem was I'd have a chance, but it's baffling me."

After downing a bowl of tomato soup and a salmon sandwich, he'd mumbled his thanks, then headed back outside. A little later she heard the heart-soaring roar of the truck's engine, but her hopes were dashed when it sputtered and died.

That had been two hours ago. Mac was still outside, still working diligently beneath the hood of the truck, but with the afternoon shadows already lengthening and darkness beginning to creep in, Eve relinquished her hopes of leaving and resigned herself to spending another night in the cabin.

To her relief Hope had slept between feedings and seemed unperturbed by the situation. Eve shifted the baby from one shoulder to the other, noting that Mac had closed the hood and was making his way up the path to the cabin.

Eve lowered Hope into her basket and covered her with one of the blankets from the bed. Going to the door, Eve opened it a crack. Mac stood on the porch stamping wet snow from his boots.

"No luck getting the truck going again?" she asked, keeping her tone light.

Mac shook his head. "None." His sigh was heartfelt. He slipped inside, and she closed the door behind him. "I've tinkered and fiddled with everything, but nothing seems to make a bit of difference." He shrugged out of his jacket and hung it on the row of hooks behind the door. "Do you know if it was running all right the last time David used it?''

"I think so," Eve replied, then frowned. "The last time David had it out was the day he died," she finished, flashing him a concerned glance.

Mac sat down on the recliner and eased off his boots. "In the message you left on my answering machine you said he'd been on his way here, to the cabin. What actually happened?" he asked.

"He drove up here every Friday and stayed overnight, coming back late Saturday. He came the same way we did, on the main highway and, according to a witness driving in the opposite direction, suddenly veered off the road and into a snow bank. By the time the other driver stopped his car and ran back, there was nothing he could do," she explained in a somber tone.

"He drove into town and reported the accident to the police. They had David's truck towed back to town where the police checked it over, but other than a dent to the front fender there didn't appear to be any major damage."

"He must have died instantly." Mac stared ahead, his voice echoing with sadness.

"The coroner's report said he'd suffered a brain aneurysm," Eve replied softly.

Mac stood up. "I'd better try and wash some of the dirt from my hands." He strode off in the direction of the bathroom.

"So we're here for another night," Eve stated calmly, when Mac returned a few minutes later.

He nodded. "I had hoped to have you and the baby at the hospital by now, getting the care you need…" his voice trailed off.

"Hope and I are fine," Eve said, touched by his concern. "Don't blame yourself."

"Ah, but I do," he countered as he moved to stand in front of the fire. "You and the baby wouldn't be in this mess if—"

"Let's not go there," she said. "We're safe and warm. And tomorrow a road crew will come along, and we'll be out of here."

"I hope you're right," he said, impressed by her attitude and her optimism. She appeared to be taking the situation in stride, or at the least, determined to put on a brave face.

Still, she had to be worried about the baby, about herself, and the possibility that they might not be rescued tomorrow. Instead of voicing her anxiety, she'd put her own fears aside and was trying to lift his spirits.

"How is Hope?" he asked, bending to peer into the basket at the foot of the bed.

"Amazing as it is, she's fine," Eve assured him.

He straightened and looked into her eyes. "And what about you, Eve? How are you holding up?"

Eve felt her heart kick against her ribs in response to the genuine concern she could see in the gray depths of his eyes. She resolutely reminded herself that the reason for her reaction had nothing to do with attraction and everything to do with the fact that her hormones were out of balance after giving birth.

She swallowed to alleviate the sudden dryness in her throat. "I'd kill for a long soak in a hot bath. In fact, I don't think I'd even mind if the water was lukewarm," she added with a smile.

Mac's deep rumble of laughter caught her by surprise and sent a delicious thrill racing through her. She joined in the laughter, amazed at the transformation she had just witnessed.

Gone were the lines of worry creasing his forehead, gone, too, the tension along his jaw. While his smile on its own had a devastating effect, the deep rich sound of his laughter was lethal. Every nerve in her body tingled with awareness, and the light dancing in his eyes took her breath away.

"I think that could be arranged," she heard him say.

Eve struggled to shake off her reaction. "I was kidding. It doesn't matter," she assured him a little breathlessly.

"Nonsense." He pointed toward the fireplace. "Do you see those pipes? They're part of the water-heating system. The fire's been burning since last night, so there should be enough hot water for a decent bath," he told her.

"Really?" Eve said excitedly. "That sounds wonderful. But the baby…"

"Is she due to wake up soon?" Mac cut in.

"Not for a while. I just finished feeding her," she replied. "She should sleep for another hour, maybe more."

"That should give you enough time, don't you think? On you go. I'll keep my eye on Hope."

Eve didn't know what to say. A bath would feel like heaven. "Are you sure?"

"Positive," came the reply.

Forty minutes later Eve climbed into the half-filled bathtub. Though the bathroom itself was chilly, the temperature of the water couldn't have been more perfect.

Using an elastic band she'd found in a drawer in the kitchen, she'd pulled her hair up into a ponytail, and as she reached for the bar of soap she sank down and let out a sigh of contentment.

She felt confident Mac could take care of the baby. After all, he'd managed very well the day before. She lingered as long as she dared and, feeling like a brand-new woman, stepped onto the bath mat and wrapped herself in one of the few remaining towels.

While waiting for the bath to fill, she'd rummaged in the bedroom closet and found a checkered flannel shirt, warm socks and a pair of jeans that had belonged to David. She'd noticed during the past two hours that her breasts had started to feel full and heavy, and she took **it as a sign** that her milk would come in soon. After putting her bra back on she slipped her arms into the flannel shirt, glad of its warmth. The jeans were too long and too wide around her waist, but she rolled up the legs and used the belt from the bathrobe to keep them from falling down.

She knew she must look a sight, the mirror above the sink told half the story, but she didn't care. It felt so good to be wearing something other than her maternity clothes or, for that matter, David's bathrobe.

She emerged half an hour later, surprised to find Mac standing with Hope in his arms, his back to the fire. A smile creased his face when he saw her. "Is that the latest fashion?" he asked, his voice laced with amusement.

Eve couldn't stop the rush of color to her cheeks. "Actually, it's called improvisation," she replied. "Was she crying? I hope I didn't take too long."

"No problem. When I peeked in the basket a few minutes ago her eyes were wide open so I thought I'd pick her up before she started to cry." He eased the baby away from his shoulder and held her out to Eve. "Here, you'd better take her."

Eve gathered the baby in her arms.

"How was your bath?"

"Wonderful."

"Good. I might have one later. But first I'll stoke up the fire." He turned and pushed the firescreen aside, before adding several logs.

Mac retreated to the kitchen, leaving Eve to feed the baby in the warmth. Glancing around, he saw that Eve already had their evening meal, a repetition of lunch, in hand. He crossed to the kitchen window, catching a glimpse of his reflection.

He ran a hand over his face, feeling the roughness of his two-day-old beard. A bath, shave and a change of clothes would be welcome, but he knew that nothing in David's closet would fit him. He'd grown taller and more muscular than his brother, and while the shirt and jeans of David's that Eve wore made her sexy and appealing, he knew he'd look ridiculous trying to fit into clothes several sizes too small.

Unwilling to return to the living room until Eve had finished feeding Hope, Mac pulled out a chair and sat down at the table. A stack of papers took up a portion of the table and, pulling them towards him, he began to leaf through them. He soon realized he'd come upon a set of plans and drawings for the proposed golf course and clubhouse.

"What are you reading?" Eve asked later as she joined him in the kitchen. She moved to the stove and turned on the heat under the pot of soup.

"Hmm?" Mac glanced up at her, obviously distracted.

"What's so interesting?" she asked.

"I found David's plans for the golf course and clubhouse," he said.

Eve smiled. "I wondered what became of them. David was so excited about those plans."

"They're quite ambitious, but he's done a great job. As far as any prospective buyer is concerned, they'll go a long way to helping us sell this piece of property."

Eve's hand stilled in the process of stirring the soup. "Who said anything about selling?" she asked, her voice as chilly as the night air. "I thought I'd made myself perfectly clear. I have no intention of selling my half of the property."

"You can't be serious," Mac replied.

"I've never been more serious in my life," she countered. She glanced over her shoulder in time to see Mac's jaw tighten with tension. "David's dream was to put those plans into operation," she went on. "I want to fulfill that dream. I would have thought you would want the same." She turned off the stove and poured soup into two bowls.

"And just how do you propose to accomplish that?" Mac asked. "From what I've seen, it'll take a great deal of money to get a project as big as this up and running. Do you have investors waiting in the wings?"

Eve made no reply. She set the empty pan in the sink and turned on the tap, realizing with a pang that she hadn't thought about what it would take to bring David's dream to fruition. It had been enough to know David had wanted to build the golf course and clubhouse and that they would be a memorial to him. Naive as she might be about the kind of resources needed, she refused to let Mac see that he had in any way dimmed her enthusiasm for the project.

In the wake of his comments and his obvious determination to dismiss his brother's dream and sell to the highest bidder, she realized Mac was just like Larry, charming and attentive when it suited him, ruthless and unfeeling when it didn't. How could she have let herself forget that Mac's sole reason for coming to Cypress Crossing was to collect his inheritance and return to Switzerland?

During the past thirty-six hours, her initial opinion had undergone a complete reversal. The cool, arrogant man she'd first encountered had been replaced by a kinder, gentler, caring one, the kind of man a woman could depend on. She'd let her guard down. Begun to believe he was worthy of David's praise. She'd been wrong.

"No matter what it takes, I'll find a way to make David's dream happen," she told him, and with that she turned and left the room.

Mac cursed under his breath as Eve walked away. He hadn't meant to sound so callous or so blunt, but he felt sure she hadn't fully realized the tremendous amount of work the project would entail. He couldn't blame her for wanting to see David's dream become a reality. It was obvious his brother had spent a good deal of time working on the plans— plans that while ambitious were also innovative and exciting.

But no matter how exciting the idea was, taking on a project the size and scope of this one would mean total involvement and a long-term commit- ment on his part. He'd want to be on hand at all times to oversee each phase of the work and to im- merse himself in the day-to-day progress, a circum- stance that would require him to move to Cypress Crossing.

Rising to the challenge would also mean contact with Eve. As half owner and partner in the project, she would she have to be consulted, and he would need her approval on any changes that might be nec- essary. He shook his head. Why was he even think- ing about it? He ignored the cry of protest that came from somewhere deep inside his heart.

Dreams were for children and fools. The sooner he sold his half of the inheritance the sooner he'd be on a plane back to Switzerland, to the quiet life that suited him, the kind of life to which he'd re- signed himself.

Chapter Nine

When Eve awoke the next morning, she stared at the ceiling and sent up a silent prayer that Mac would fix the truck or the road-clearing crews would find them today.

Throughout the night the baby had awakened every two hours. Around two in the morning she'd felt a strange sensation deep inside her breasts just before her milk began to flow. At first the baby had been surprised and a little upset by the new development, then she'd nestled against Eve's breast, hungrily enjoying the warm milk.

During those wakeful times, Eve found her thoughts returning to the confrontation with Mac, and each time, she was besieged by a variety of emotions ranging from anger to sadness to disappointment. Anger that Mac had assumed she would agree to sell the property, sadness that he hadn't cared for his brother enough to want to make David's dream come true, and disappointment that he couldn't see his brother's legacy as a way to keep David's memory alive.

Eve glanced over at the recliner, but Mac wasn't there. Her breasts felt full and tight, a clear indication she needed to feed the baby. Reaching over, she pulled the basket closer. It was empty. For a fleeting moment panic seized her. But before she could move or react, the sound of footsteps in the hallway captured her attention.

Mac appeared in the doorway with Hope in his arms.

"Were you looking for your daughter?" he asked with a smile. "She was awake, so I thought I'd change her for you and let you enjoy a few extra minutes of sleep."

"Thank you," she said, touched by his thoughtfulness, but determined not to let him see it.

Mac crossed to the sofa bed and deposited the baby in her arms.

"I've already stoked up the fire so it should be good for a while and there's hot water on the stove if you need it," he told her as he straightened. "I'll be outside working on the truck. If I can't get it going, I'm going to make my way out to the main road and look for the road crew."

* * *

By noon Eve was growing increasingly worried. Mac hadn't succeeded in getting the truck started, and it had been more than an hour since she'd seen him trudge down the road toward the turn off.

When she heard the sound of an engine, she hurried to the window in time to see a large snowplow lumbering into sight, its enormous blades cutting through the deep snow, tossing it aside with ease.

It was all Eve could do not to race outside and cheer. From her vantage point at the window she watched Mac jump down off the plow's running board and stride up to the cabin.

"They've radioed for an ambulance and a tow truck," Mac said when he reached her. "They'll be here in an hour, maybe a little longer."

"An ambulance?" Eve repeated in surprise.

"Yes. I thought it best in the circumstances," he told her. "You'll be taken straight to the hospital, where you and the baby can be checked over thoroughly."

"But what about you? How will you get back to town?" she asked.

"I'll get a ride with the tow truck driver," he said.

"I'd better feed the baby before the ambulance gets here." She turned away.

"Eve..."

Her name on his lips sent a shiver through her as she faced him once more.

"I wanted to say I'm sorry about last night. Sorry that I upset you," he said.

A mixture of surprise and pleasure at his apology danced along her nerves. "That's okay. I just think it would be a mistake to—"

"Let's not get into that now. We'll have plenty of opportunity to discuss it later," he said. "There're a few things I need to take care of before the tow truck gets here."

"All right," Eve said, hiding her disappointment, but acknowledging that this wasn't the time to try to hash out the problem.

It was well past seven by the time Mac made his way back to the condo. After the tow truck driver had dropped him and David's truck at the garage, he'd spoken briefly to the mechanic before heading for the condo and a long, hot shower.

He'd contemplated taking a taxi to the hospital to check on Eve and the baby, but he'd promised her he would call in at the inn and talk to the staff. At the inn, he'd introduced himself to the receptionist, then asked her to round up the staff currently on duty. She'd done as he asked, suggesting they gather in the small private banquet room on the first floor.

Once he'd introduced himself, he'd explained that he and Eve were now business partners. He'd also told them Eve had had her baby, quickly assuring them mother and baby were doing well. From the general murmurings, he could tell they were rather curious about him. He'd offered to answer questions, and after a brief exchange, they'd returned to work.

Now Mac stood at the crosswalk waiting for the light to change. Not for the first time since he'd watched the ambulance drive away from the cabin he found his thoughts turning to Eve and Hope.

It came as something of a shock to realize how much he missed them. A feeling of friendship had sprung up between him and Eve during their time at the cabin. They'd been getting on well, until he'd made the comment that David's plans would prove valuable in helping them find a buyer.

He supposed her adverse reaction shouldn't have surprised him. He found her loyalty to David commendable. But Mac hoped that in time she would realize what an enormous undertaking building a golf course and clubhouse would be and that using David's plans to help sell the property made more sense.

Mac crossed the street and let himself into the condo. Closing the door behind him, he moved to the stairs. The sound of a baby crying stopped him in his tracks.

Surely Eve and Hope hadn't been discharged from the hospital already? The cry came again, louder this time. Mac retraced his steps and before he could think twice he knocked on Eve's door.

Positive that his knock had been drowned out by the baby's cries, he raised his hand to knock again when the door opened.

Eve, wearing a blue shirt and navy slacks, her shoulder-length hair drawn back in a ponytail that made her look all of sixteen, stood in the doorway the baby in her arms.

"You are home," he said. "I couldn't believe it when I heard the baby crying. I thought you'd have to spend the night at the hospital."

Eve shook her head. "The doctors checked us both over and gave us a clean bill of health, so I asked if I could take her home," she replied as she transferred the crying baby from one arm to the other.

"I'd better let you go," he said, relieved to know they were both fine. "If there's anything I can do, anything you need, just let me know," he added, thinking she looked a little frazzled.

"Actually…" Eve began then shook her head.

"What?"

"I hate to impose. You've done so much already." She lifted Hope against her shoulder, patting the baby's back in an attempt to soothe her.

"What can I do?" Mac asked, the thought of sitting upstairs on his own having little appeal.

"I should have brought the bed you made back

with me," she told him. "Ever since I got home I've been trying to put her crib together. Now she's hungry, and it's still in pieces on the bedroom floor."

"Why don't I tackle the crib while you feed her," Mac suggested.

A look of relief crossed her face. "Oh, would you?" She took a step back, and he followed. "I had planned to have everything ready for the baby this weekend."

"Where's the crib?" he asked.

"In my bedroom." She nodded toward the door on her right.

"Go feed your daughter," he said.

Eve flashed a smile of gratitude before she turned away.

Mac entered Eve's bedroom and dropped his jacket on the bed. The room was tidy except for the pieces of the baby's crib strewn over the floor. A quick glance around at the pink walls, the pale-green carpet and the plain but stylish bedroom furniture told him Eve had simple but classic tastes.

Atop the light-oak dresser opposite the bed sat a pile of neatly folded baby clothes. The matching oak dressing table had been cleared of personal items and transformed into a changing table. Mac smiled, admiring her resourcefulness.

Picking up the screwdriver, he set to work. The scent of baby powder mingled with a decidedly more feminine perfume that reminded him of the wildflowers that grew near his home in the Alps.

Half an hour later he tightened the last of the screws. Lifting the mattress he found leaning against the wall, he dropped it into place. As he stood back to survey his efforts he found his thoughts turning to Hope's father. Who was he? he wondered. And more to the point, where was he? Didn't he realize how much Eve and the baby needed him? If they were *his* family, he'd never leave them....

Mac frowned. Where had that absurd notion come from? Eve and Hope weren't his family and never would be. And besides, he wasn't in any way qualified to be a parent.

"Oh, you've done it! Thank you," Eve said, breaking into his wayward thoughts. "Would you hold her for a moment while I put a cover and sheet on the mattress?"

Before he had time to reply, she'd handed him the sleeping baby. Gazing down at Hope, wrapped snugly in a blanket decorated with tiny animals, Mac felt the familiar tug at his heart.

Her size amazed him. He touched the tiny fist curled against her cheek. How could anyone abandon a helpless baby? Had his mother cried the day she left him on the hospital steps? Had her choice to give him up been made out of desperation, maybe even out of love?

Maggie Kingston had tried to tell him that he

shouldn't judge or jump to conclusions about the choice his mother made. Back then he'd been an angry, sullen, teenager, unwilling to listen to any explanation that might put things in a different or more positive light. He'd stubbornly stuck to the belief that his mother hadn't loved him, hadn't wanted him, but now he realized, with a pang of conscience, that he might have been wrong.

"You're so good with her, so relaxed," said Eve as she turned to him once more. "I bet she knows it's you."

"Surely not," Mac said, strangely thrilled at the idea Hope might know him.

"You'd be surprised how much babies can sense," Eve replied. "Would you put her down for me?"

Mac did as she asked, gently depositing Hope in her crib.

Eve tucked a blanket around her. "She should sleep for a few hours," she said as they withdrew. "Oh, by the way, how did things go at the inn? I probably should have introduced you to everyone the other morning. I hope you didn't have any problems."

"None," he replied. "They were surprised to hear you'd had the baby, of course, and more than a bit curious about me, especially when I told them I'd be taking over until you were able to return to work." He stopped. "There I go making assumptions. You are planning to take some time off before going back to work, aren't you?''

He watched Eve's expression grow thoughtful. ''I'm not sure what I'm going to do. David said I should take six weeks' maternity leave. Now that he's gone, I'm not sure what to do.''

''Hire a manager,'' Mac said.

Eve darted him a frowning glance. ''I'll have to think about that.'' She opened the fridge and removed a carton of milk. ''I'm going to make some hot chocolate. Care to join me?''

Mac hesitated, caught off guard by the invitation. They'd spent the past two nights stranded in a cabin forced to spend time together, and now that they were back in town, he'd expected her to be less than anxious to spend any more time with him.

''Don't you like hot chocolate?'' Eve broke into his scattered thoughts.

''I love hot chocolate,'' he replied, recalling that he'd tasted the sweet treat for the very first time the Christmas he'd spent at the Kingstons'.

A flood of forgotten memories swept over him. Maggie Kingston had asked him the very same question, and when he'd blurted out that he'd never tasted hot chocolate before, he'd been sure she would laugh at him. She hadn't laughed. Instead she'd ruffled his hair in a gesture of affection before setting the mug of chocolate, one of many she'd made for him that Christmas, in front of him.

"Mac?"

"Sorry. Yes, hot chocolate sounds wonderful." He approached the counter. "Do you have any marshmallows?"

Eve grinned and held up a bag of miniature marshmallows. "Hot chocolate with marshmallows was a Christmas tradition at our house, one of the few my parents indulged in. What about you?"

"Maggie made hot chocolate a bedtime treat every night during the Christmas season," Mac heard himself say.

"Maggie?" Eve repeated with a frown. "You must mean David's mother—your adopted mother," she said, noticing the sad expression that had flitted across his features during the lengthy silence.

Mac nodded.

Behind her the microwave beeped telling her the two mugs of milk she'd placed inside were hot. Eve scooped several spoonfuls of powdered chocolate mix into the mugs and stirred the mixture before adding a handful of marshmallows. She slid the mug across the counter to Mac.

"Thanks." Lifting the mug, he inhaled the sweet scent of chocolate and marshmallows.

"Let's sit down," Eve invited, and carried her mug to the love seat.

Mac chose the chair. "I'd forgotten how delicious it tastes," he said after taking a sip.

Eve smiled. "So tell me about your adoptive parents. What were they like?"

Mac took another sip before answering. "Maggie and Joe Kingston were two of the finest people I ever knew." His voice vibrated with emotion, and Eve felt tears sting her eyes at the love she could hear there.

"How did you meet them?" she asked.

For a long moment Mac said nothing. "I'd just turned thirteen and I'd been assigned to yet another caseworker," he began. "Mrs. McManus was new to the job, and I'd been passed on to her because..." He stopped, astonished to find himself relating the story.

Whenever people brought up the subject of his past, he usually deflected their questions by turning the tables and asking them about their families. It was his experience, given the choice, people preferred to talk about themselves.

"Because?" Eve prompted.

He met her interested gaze. "You don't really want to hear this," he told her. "Why don't you tell me about your parents," he said in an attempt to divert her.

Eve's blue eyes held him hostage. "I do want to hear it," she said, and there was no mistaking the sincerity in her tone.

No one had ever rejected the opportunity to talk about their own life before, and the door to the deepest part of his heart where he kept his happiest memories opened a crack.

"You were passed on to Mrs. McManus because…?" Eve tried again.

"Because I was a pain in the butt and all the other social workers had given up on me," he told her.

"Oh."

"Mrs. McManus turned out to be the best thing that happened to me," Mac continued. "She was determined I would have a memorable Christmas, and so she said she'd found a family willing to take me in. On a trial basis, of course." He came to a halt.

Over the next hour Mac found himself telling Eve things he'd never told another living soul, not even David. In turn, Eve told him how lonely and frightening it had been to have parents who ignored her.

For the first time in his life Mac learned that while his early years had been difficult and often painful, being part of a family wasn't necessarily all it was cracked up to be.

"My goal is to make sure Hope always knows how much I love her. I never want her to feel lonely or afraid," Eve said, a steely determination in her voice. "But I can't help worrying…" She hurried on. "I mean, I've done some baby-sitting, but I don't know the first thing about being a mother, about parenting." She sighed.

"From what I've seen so far you're doing just fine," Mac commented, and was rewarded with a smile.

"Thanks," Eve said. "And as for you, you must have spent time around babies yourself."

Mac frowned. "What makes you say that?"

"There are some men who are petrified of even picking up a newborn, but not you."

"Thanks," he said, warmed by her praise. "But that doesn't mean I'd make a good parent."

"True. Though from what you've told me about Maggie and Joe Kingston, all you need to do is follow their example."

Mac pondered this for a moment, but before he could comment, Eve spoke again.

"What's your best memory of the time you spent with them?" she asked.

"That's easy," Mac replied. "Maggie would read me a story every night. No one had ever read a bedtime story to me before," he told her, the memory bringing warmth to his voice. "That first Christmas she read *The Adventures of Huckleberry Finn.* After Maggie turned out the light, David would come to my room and read another chapter."

Eve smiled. "David was always thoughtful and kind," she said, and without warning she burst into tears.

Startled and concerned, Mac rose from the chair and moved to sit next to Eve on the love seat. He was at a loss, and the sound of her sobs tore at his heart. Sliding his arm around her shoulder he pulled her into his arms. Her hair felt like silk, and with each breath he took, the scent of wildflowers stirred his senses, arousing emotions he'd taught himself not to feel.

Eve's crying eased at last, and she lifted her head

to look at him. Mac handed her several tissues from the box on the coffee table, and she blew her nose.

"I'm sorry. I don't know what came over me," she said, her eyes still glistening with moisture. "David was a wonderful friend. I miss him."

"I miss him, too." Mac brought his left hand to her face, tenderly wiping away a stray tear with his thumb.

Eve gazed unblinking at him, her tear-stained face inches from his own, and before he could think about the consequences, he closed the gap between them.

Her mouth tasted of salt with a lingering trace of chocolate. But stronger and more potent was the warmth and natural sweetness that was the true essence of Eve.

Mac's mouth felt soft and warm against her own, sending shivers of delight through her. She'd never been kissed with such tenderness or such reverence, and behind her eyelids she felt fresh tears gather.

She moaned in invitation not in protest, opening her mouth to offer him better access. At first his tongue made teasing forays into hers, then as she joined in the erotic dance, his kiss became more urgent, and the moan she heard came from somewhere deep in his throat.

His arms tightened around her, crushing her against him, and his mouth devoured hers, making her light-headed with a need that left her aching. She'd never been kissed like this before, so thoroughly, so wantonly.

Whenever Larry kissed her, she'd tasted *his* hunger, *his* desire, never her own. Larry hadn't bothered to make any conscious effort to ensure her satisfaction.

With one earthshaking kiss, Mac had brought her to instant arousal. Even more powerful was the realization that with one kiss he'd touched her soul, leaving her with a strong sense of rightness, of belonging, of coming home.

Without warning, it was over, and Mac was holding her away from him. She glimpsed a look of confusion on his face before his expression became unreadable.

"I'm sorry. I had no right. That was a mistake." Releasing her, he stood up.

Pain clutched her heart at the regret she could hear in his voice. But before she could say anything, the baby started to cry.

"Thanks for the hot chocolate. If you get me my coat, I'll see myself out. Oh, and don't worry about the inn," he said as he followed her to the bedroom. "I'll look after things for the next few days, until you decide what you want to do."

Chapter Ten

During the days leading up to Christmas, Eve saw little of Mac. She heard him leave early each morning and return late at night. That he was deliberately avoiding her seemed the only explanation for his behavior, and Eve tried to convince herself she wasn't hurt or disappointed.

She'd managed to get Hope on a four-hour feeding schedule, and more often than not Eve would nap while the baby slept.

At odd times she'd found her thoughts returning to those moments in Mac's arms. The tears she'd shed had come from nowhere, but on reflection she acknowledged that since learning of David's death she hadn't really cried, hadn't truly grieved for him until that moment.

What had started out as comfort had escalated into arousal of an intensity she'd never expected. The kiss had been an awakening for her, and when Mac pulled away, she'd caught the desire in his eyes before the shutters came down.

She reminded herself she wasn't in the market for a relationship, wasn't sure after her dismal experience with Larry that she'd ever trust a man again. Besides, she had a new and far more important responsibility to consider, her daughter, Hope.

Mac was a loner, and not the kind of man who'd be interested in a permanent relationship or, for that matter, willing to take on another man's child. It would be foolish to forget that his primary concern was selling his half of David's estate and returning to Switzerland.

With only a few days left till Christmas, Eve decided to go shopping. She'd received a call from Alison, the inn's receptionist, reminding Eve of the children's annual Christmas party planned for later that afternoon and asking her to stop by and check over the final arrangements. Everyone at the inn was anxious to see Eve and the baby.

Eve had promised to drop in as soon as she'd finished shopping. After dressing the baby warmly, Eve pulled on her hooded jacket, boots and gloves and set out for the stores. It felt good to be out in the crisp winter air, and as she pushed the baby stroller down Main Street several friends and acquaintances stopped to chat and admire the baby.

The local businesses had their windows adorned with brightly colored lights, Christmas trees and simple Nativity scenes. Eve spent an enjoyable hour popping in and out of a variety of stores, picking up a few groceries and some last-minute gifts.

When she arrived at the inn, Alison came around the desk to greet her.

"There you are," Alison said with a smile. "Everyone has been dying to see the baby, and you, too, of course."

"How is everything here?" Eve asked as she removed the quilted cover from the baby's stroller.

"Hectic, as always, but we're managing," Alison replied as she peered into the stroller. "Oh, Eve, she's beautiful! What's her name?"

"Hope Elizabeth Darling," Eve replied with pride.

"That's a beautiful name," Alison said. "We were all thrilled to hear about the baby, but you could have knocked us over with a feather when Mac Kingston made the announcement that you and he are co-owners of the inn. The staff I've talked to are pleased and relieved at the news," she confessed. "We were afraid the place would be sold and we'd lose our jobs…

"Oops, I'd better get back to work," Alison continued after a quick glance at the reception desk where several people stood waiting. "The party committee is at work getting the restaurant ready for later. I told them you were coming," she added as she hurried away.

Eve pushed the stroller toward the restaurant. She felt relieved that the news of her new status at the inn had been received so positively, and she vowed to do her best to keep things running smoothly through the next transition, when Mac sold his half interest.

Ignoring the sign on the restaurant door that read, Closed for a Private Party, Eve maneuvered the stroller through the swinging door. Inside, the small group of staff setting tables for the party stopped what they were doing and turned to greet her.

"Eve! Hi! Alison said you were dropping by," said Becky, one of the waitresses, as she came toward her.

"Hi! It looks like you have everything under control," Eve said.

Everyone clamored around for a peek at the baby and to offer congratulations.

"By the way, did you remember to find someone to play Santa?" Becky asked. In previous years David had played the role, enjoying it immensely.

"I asked Jack Holden," Eve said. "I thought I told you."

"You did," Melanie, another waitress, replied. "But Jack's mother had an emergency operation in

Vancouver so he decided to take his family there for Christmas. Didn't he tell you?''

"Yes, he did,'' Eve said, realizing she'd forgotten all about it. "I'm sorry. It slipped my mind.''

"The kids will be disappointed if there's no Santa,'' Sally said.

"It won't be easy finding someone at the last minute,'' Melanie commented.

"Why don't you ask your new business partner?'' Sally suggested. "He'd look terrific in a Santa suit.''

"I don't know,'' Eve said hesitatingly, not at all sure Mac would relish the idea.

"What have you got to lose?'' Sally asked.

Eve could see they were serious. "All right. I'll go upstairs now and ask him.''

She hadn't seen Mac since the night he'd kissed her, and as she rode the elevator to the mezzanine, feelings of apprehension and excitement swamped her. The elevator doors opened, and she pushed the stroller into the hallway leading to hers and David's offices. As she drew near her office she heard Mac's familiar deep voice.

"And you're right,'' he was saying. "The real estate market is good at the moment. Selling my half of the properties shouldn't take long. And the sooner I find a buyer the sooner I'll be out of here.''

Eve's heart skidded to a halt, and her breath caught in her throat. While she'd known from the beginning Mac intended to sell the inn and leave

Cypress Crossing, hearing him confirm it elicited sadness and disappointment she hadn't expected to feel. Taking several steadying breaths, she noisily nudged the office door open with the stroller and entered.

Mac met her gaze and for a second an emotion she couldn't decipher flashed in his eyes.

"Gotta run. I'll talk to you later," he said before hanging up the phone. "Eve, this is a surprise." He rose to his feet. "What brings you here?"

Before she could answer, the phone on her desk rang. Mac sighed. "I came through to your office to look for a file, and the phone hasn't stopped ringing since," he said as he reached for the receiver.

Eve maneuvered the stroller to the other side of her desk. Hope stirred but didn't awaken.

"I'm sorry, I didn't catch your name," Mac said, drawing Eve's attention to the conversation. "Mrs. Portmann. Yes, it was a shock. Thank you. My brother will indeed be missed." Mac fell silent.

"Sorry? Did you say you want to speak to Eve Darling?" His gaze darted to Eve a question in his eyes.

Eve nodded and moved closer.

"Please hold for a moment, and I'll get her for you." Mac handed Eve the phone.

"Hello, Mrs. Portmann," Eve said in a cheerful tone.

"And the best of the season to you, too. I trust

your suite is in order and you have everything you need.''

Eve listened to the lady's reply, aware all the while of Mac standing nearby. He made no move to return to David's office and give her privacy, but stood waiting and watching.

"Of course. I'd be happy to," she assured Mrs. Portmann. "Oh, you mean now?" She hesitated. "Ah, fine, I'll be right there."

"And who, pray tell, is Mrs. Portmann?" Mac asked when she hung up.

"She's a valued customer," Eve told him. "She lives in Vancouver but has family here in Cypress Crossing. Every Christmas and Easter she pays them a visit.

"She stays at the inn, often for two weeks or more. And over the course of her stay she treats her relatives to one or two meals at the restaurant. We try to cater to her as much as we can."

"I see," Max said. "And what's so urgent that she wants to see you now?"

"She's made a reservation for a dinner party on Boxing Day and wants to go over the menu," she explained.

"Wouldn't it make more sense to talk to the chef?"

"She has," Eve told him. "She's a bit of a worrywart and likes to go over a few of the minor details with me. It'll take ten minutes, fifteen at the most. Could you keep your eye on Hope till I get back?''

Mac darted an anxious glance at the stroller.

"She's not due to be fed for another hour," Eve assured him, already halfway to the door.

"All right," he said, seconds before Eve slipped out the door.

Mac raked his hand through his hair and let out a sigh. For the past few days he'd succeeded in avoiding Eve and the baby. He'd told himself it was for the best, that just because he'd helped bring Hope into the world didn't mean mother and daughter were his responsibility or concern. As soon as he found a buyer for his half of David's legacy, he planned to be on the first plane back to Switzerland and his quiet, normal life.

Not for the first time his thoughts shifted to the last time he'd seen Eve, more specifically to the kiss they'd shared. He hadn't been able to get the taste of her, the scent of her, the feel of her lips opening like a flower beneath his, out of his head. The kiss had shaken him to the core, eliciting a response that had left him restless and aching, not just for sexual fulfillment, but for something far deeper. What? He had no idea.

Added to that had been the eerie sensation of how right, how perfect she'd felt in his arms. He'd never wanted to let her go. It had been these stunning revelations that had sent him running. He couldn't al-

low himself to care too much, couldn't afford to let
his guard down, not for a minute, because the end
result would be the same.

Throughout his life everyone he'd cared about or
loved had abandoned him in one way or another,
and he'd long since decided never to open his heart
to that kind of pain again.

Besides, there was the baby's father to consider.
What if he came back? And, anyway, Mac knew
nothing about raising children or about being the
kind of father Hope deserved.

Behind him Mac heard muffled sounds coming
from the stroller. He moved around the desk to
check the baby. His breath caught in his throat when
he saw those startling blue eyes, so like Eve's, staring up at him.

Captivated, he smiled.

"Hello, little one. How are you? I've missed
you," he said, surprising himself as he said it.

When her tiny mouth curved into what he felt sure
was an answering smile, an emotion he refused to
acknowledge curled around his heart.

But her smile quickly faded and her expression
changed as her pretty face scrunched up.

"No… Please, don't cry," he pleaded. But she
ignored his request and began to howl.

Mac bent over the stroller. Reaching in, he slid
his hand under her back and lifted her into his arms.

"Hey! I do believe you've gained a little weight

since the last time I held you,'' Mac commented as he settled her comfortably against his shoulder, rubbing her back the way he'd seen Eve do.

Much to his relief the baby's cries ceased. Did she recognize his voice, he wondered, remembering Eve's comment that Hope knew him. Warmth spread through him at the thought.

Shifting his weight from one foot to the other, he rocked her. The sweet scent of baby, mingling with a hint of the flowery perfume Eve wore, assailed him. He closed his eyes and inhaled deeply, intent on imprinting the scent on his memory so he would be able to recall and relive these precious moments.

Hope moved her head, and his mouth brushed her ear. He kissed it tenderly, amazed at its perfection. His lips grazed her soft cheek, then he kissed her button nose, careful not to scratch her with the roughness of his jaw.

Fearful she might start crying again he continued the rocking motion, basking in the wonder and warmth sweeping through him and entwining his heart. When she began to wriggle, and her tiny mouth made wet sucking noises against his neck, he didn't know what to do.

Eve had said she'd only be gone ten or fifteen minutes. How long it had it been since she'd left? Was that the elevator? Mac held his breath and listened, but all he heard were the faint strains of a Christmas carol coming from downstairs.

Desperate to keep Hope from crying, he began to sing.

When Eve walked off the elevator minutes later, she heard the deep melodious sound of someone singing "The Little Drummer Boy." She slowed as she approached the doorway of her office, and her heart melted at the tender scene.

He looked so natural, so right, holding Hope against his broad chest, rocking her, and for a moment Eve allowed herself to fantasize and to imagine Mac was the baby's father, that they were a real family.

Tears stung her eyes. She blinked them away, angry at indulging in such foolishness, remembering with a pang the conversation she'd overheard when she'd arrived earlier.

"Did she wake up already?" Eve's question brought an abrupt end to Mac's song, and he turned to her.

"Ah, yes," he replied, feeling his cheeks grow warm under her gaze.

"Did you take care of Mrs. Portmann?" Mac asked, easing Hope from his shoulder and handing her to her mother.

"Yes," Eve assured him. "Everything is under control. By the way, I almost forgot the reason I came up here. I need to ask a favor."

"A favor?" Mac repeated with a frown.

"Yes. There's a staff children's party this afternoon."

"Children's party?"

"We do it every Christmas. It's for those staff members who have children," she explained. "It starts at three. Every year David played Santa for the kids."

"You mean my brother dressed up in a Santa suit?" Mac sounded surprised and amused.

"Yes, and I wondered if you'd like to do the honors this year."

"You can't be serious," Mac replied, stunned she would even ask. "Surely there's someone else willing to take on the job."

"We did have someone lined up, but he had a family emergency and had to change his plans," she explained. "It's only for an hour or two. The children look forward to it, and they'll be so disappointed if Santa doesn't show up."

Mac shook his head. "I've never...I wouldn't know what to do. Besides the costume probably won't fit," he finished lamely, a hint of desperation in his voice.

"The costume is a one-size-fits-all, so that shouldn't be a problem. The gifts for the children were bought and wrapped weeks ago. Playing Santa is easy, you just say a few ho-ho-ho's when you arrive, and as you hand out the gifts you ask the children what they want for Christmas," she continued matter-of-factly.

Mac still said nothing.

"If you won't do it for me," Eve went on. "Do it for David. Please." Eve knew she wasn't being fair, but she felt sure David would have supported the idea of Mac taking his place at the party.

Mac met her gaze, the silence stretching between them.

"I'm sorry, I really don't—" Mac began but Hope interrupted him with a cry.

"Shh," Eve murmured to the baby, hiding her disappointment at Mac's refusal as she turned away. She'd been wrong to try to pressure him. Perhaps she could get one of the cooks to play the part.

"I'd better take her home." Eve lowered Hope into the stroller and tucked the quilt around her. "I'll see if I can find someone else." Picking up her jacket, she put it on and started to push the stroller toward the door.

"All right, I'll do it," Mac said with obvious reluctance.

Startled and pleased, Eve turned and met his gaze. "Thank you," she said, her tone sincere. "You'll find the Santa costume in a box in the bottom of the old filing cabinet in the corner of David's office."

Mac nodded. "And what time should I...should Santa make his appearance?"

"Four o'clock would be perfect," Eve said.

"Come through the kitchen. I'll make sure the sack of presents is waiting for you."

Mac gazed at his reflection in the mirror of the men's room. Gazing back at him he saw a white-haired, white-bearded man wearing a bright-red snowsuit trimmed with white, a scowl on his face.

He muttered under his breath, knowing it was only Eve's comment about David that had prompted him to agree to play the part of Santa. He was fast regretting his rash decision. The bulky costume made him sweat, and beneath the wig and beard he'd started to itch. The temptation to rip everything off and bid a hasty retreat almost overwhelmed him, but he quashed it.

He checked the corridor, relieved to find it empty. Eve had said he should make his appearance around four. It must be past that now, he thought, but he'd removed his watch and tucked it in the pocket of his jacket now hanging in the closet in David's office.

As quickly as the big black boots he wore would allow, Mac descended the back stairs to the kitchen. He slipped inside and stood for a moment surveying the scene. Several heads turned to look at him, each one flashing a cheerful smile and a wave.

He spotted the big red cloth bag, bursting with packages, near the door leading out to the restaurant. With a sigh he lumbered across the kitchen to heft the bag onto his back. From the other side of the door he could hear the sound of children's excited voices. Peering through the small window, he surveyed the scene.

Boys and girls of varying ages dressed in party clothes sat at the tables eating hot dogs, pizzas, cakes and cookies and drinking sodas. He recognized a number of the inn's staff members chatting at another table.

Before he could think about changing his mind, he pushed the door open and stepped into the room. At first no one appeared to notice his arrival.

"Children! Look who's come to pay us a visit." Eve's voice echoed around the room, and he glanced to his left in time to see her walking toward him.

Loud squeals of excitement from the children followed her announcement.

There was no going back.

"Relax," Eve whispered, obviously picking up on his nervousness. "They're just kids."

Mac gazed at the sea of faces staring up at him with wide-eyed wonder. His mouth felt as dry as the cloth bag on his shoulder, not for the first time since donning the Santa suit, he wished himself a thousand miles away.

"A few ho-ho-ho's would go down well about now," Eve suggested sotto voce.

Beneath the beard Mac tried to comply. "Ho..." he croaked. He cleared his throat. "Ho! Ho! Ho!

And a very Merry Christmas to everyone!'' This time the greeting came out in a booming voice.

His words were met with whoops of delight and a smattering of applause. Mac smiled, his nervousness vanishing.

Moments later he found himself seated in the corner next to a small Christmas tree, the sack of toys beside him, while the children, guided by several adults, began to form an orderly line.

An hour and a half later, Mac dug into the sack and brought out one of the few remaining presents. His thighs were numb, his legs cramping and his back aching, but he couldn't remember a time he'd enjoyed himself more.

Six-year-old Mandy Mitchell, a pretty red-haired girl with glasses, had just told him she wanted a computer game for Christmas. Then she'd kissed his cheek and slid from his knee, gripping the present he'd just given her.

"That's everyone," said Eve, who'd appeared at his side.

"There's still a couple of presents in the bag," he said, surprised by the feeling of disappointment now that his job was over.

"Better too many than not enough," Eve said. "It's time for you to leave."

"Already?" Mac said. "Do you want me to sneak out?" he asked.

Eve laughed. "I doubt that's possible with all

these children watching your every move,'' she said. ''You'd better do a quick circuit of the room, say goodbye, then head back through the kitchen. We'll keep the children occupied until you get safely upstairs.''

''Right.'' Ignoring the stiffness in his legs and back, Mac eased himself to his feet. He began to make his way around the room. Eve watched several parents stop and shake his hand.

Remembering how nervous he'd looked when he'd first appeared, Eve had to admire the way he'd handled himself. He'd spent several minutes with each child, listening attentively while they told him what they wanted for Christmas. He'd even coaxed a smile from shy little Tamara Collins, before handing her a gift from his sack. And if she wasn't mistaken, she had a suspicion Mac had enjoyed himself as much as the kids. He'd make a terrific father, she thought.

''Your new business partner did a great job. He'll make a great father.'' Startled to hear her own thoughts spoken aloud, Eve turned to find Alison Redding behind her.

''Yes,'' Eve managed to say.

''Look at Becky.'' Alison said with a soft chuckle. ''She's such a flirt. Her divorce isn't through yet, but she doesn't let that stop her.''

Eve followed Alison's smiling gaze to where Becky, a striking blonde with an eye-popping figure,

had her arm through Santa's. Mac was smiling, obviously enjoying the attention. And when Becky
leaned forward to plant a kiss on Santa's cheek, Eve
felt a pain stab at her heart, a pain she recognized
as jealousy.

Fool! She berated herself. When it came to falling
in love, why did she have to pick the wrong kind
of man?

Eve gasped. Had she just admitted she'd fallen in
love with Mac Kingston?

Chapter Eleven

"Eve, are you all right?" Alison asked. "You've gone as white as the snow."

Eve forced a smile. "I'm fine," she lied. "A little tired. I think it's time I fetched Hope and went home."

"What are you doing for Christmas?" Alison asked.

"I didn't make any plans. I assumed I'd be in the hospital having the baby," she answered, scanning the room for Millie, the head housekeeper, who'd commandeered Hope as soon as Eve arrived.

"Ron and I are having my parents and my brother and his family over for dinner," Alison said. "You're welcome to join us."

"Thank you, that's very kind of you," Eve said,

warmed by the invitation. "But I'm still adjusting to motherhood and thought I'd just spend a quiet day with the baby."

"Sounds heavenly," Alison replied. "My brother has four boys, and when they get together with our two, well, it's bedlam," she said in an affectionate tone.

Eve smiled again, thinking how wonderful it would be to have the noise and bustle of a large family around at Christmas. Growing up, she'd longed for a brother or sister to play with and to share things with.

"Looks like Santa might need rescuing." Alison nodded to where Mac, with Becky hanging on to his arm, was on his way to the kitchen.

"I'm sure he can take care of himself," Eve said, ignoring the pain squeezing her heart, because as far as she could see Mac didn't appear to be making any attempt to free himself from Becky's clutches.

"I need to find Millie," Eve said, eager now to make her escape. "Ah, here she is," she said as Millie walked over with Hope in her arms.

"Has she been good?" Eve asked, taking the baby from Millie.

"She's been wonderful. A wee treasure, just like Amanda my granddaughter," Millie said with a sigh.

Twenty minutes later Eve wheeled the stroller outside. Gigantic snowflakes, the size of maple leaves, drifted down from the night sky. As Eve headed down the path she heard a shout.

"Eve! Wait! It's slippery out here. I'll give you a hand."

At the sound of Mac's voice, her heart plummeted. He was the last person she wanted to see right now, especially if Becky was still hanging on his arm. A quick glance over her shoulder told her he was alone, and she felt her pulse skip a beat.

"Let me take the stroller," he offered, edging her aside. "Grab my arm." He stuck out his elbow and flashed a smile.

"Thanks." Eve slid her gloved hand around his arm. At the contact, warmth spread through her. They continued down the path, and Eve found herself thinking that anyone seeing them might assume they were a real family out for an evening stroll.

"The party went well. You did a great job," Eve said, wanting to fill the silence.

His smile appeared again. "I enjoyed myself."

"The children did, too."

"Thanks," he said as they came to a halt at the curb.

The light changed in their favor, and Mac pushed the stroller onto the quiet street.

"What are your plans for Christmas day?" he asked.

"I'm staying home with the baby. Why?"

They were approaching the door. "Have you got your keys handy?" Mac asked.

"In my pocket," Eve said and dug into her jacket.

Once they were inside, Mac brushed snow from his hair, then met her gaze. "If you don't have plans for Christmas I'd like to invite you to have dinner with me," he said as he began to unbutton his coat. "Hope, too, of course."

"You're going to cook Christmas dinner?" Eve said, unable to hide her surprise.

A look of amusement danced in Mac's eyes, sending her heart into a tailspin. "Not exactly. I thought I'd ask Chef Mitchell if he would put together a couple of turkey dinners with all the trimmings for us. What do you say?"

Eve hesitated. While shopping earlier she'd picked up a small chicken she'd planned to roast on Christmas. But Mac's invitation sounded much more appealing.

"Thanks, I'd like that," she said at last. "Would it be all right if we ate downstairs? That way I can put Hope to bed in her crib."

"Sure," he replied.

"I don't have a tree this year," she said with regret. "I'd planned to pick one up today, but I ran out of time. I did have a look in the tree lot next to the grocery store, but all the good ones were gone."

"That's too bad," Mac said. "What time would you like to eat?"

"Is six or six-thirty all right?" Eve asked.

"Sounds fine. I'll see you then."

Eve spent Christmas Eve cleaning house. The temptation to run out and buy one of the rather be-draggled Christmas trees she'd seen the other day was strong, but in the end she opted to string a row of lights around the pictures on her wall. She also grouped different-colored ornaments, strategically placing them throughout the room.

Christmas morning brought with it a fresh layer of snow. Eve spent the better part of the day trying to soothe a cranky, fretful baby. Hope didn't have a temperature, but she'd hardly slept all day. Eve worried the baby was coming down with a cold or worse.

By half past five, exhausted from crying, Hope finally fell sleep. Though Eve would have liked to have a nap herself, she spent the time setting the tiny table in the kitchen.

She'd called Mac earlier, telling him the baby was having a bad day and suggesting it would be best to forget dinner. He'd argued that he'd already ordered the meal and reminded her that it would be less work for her in the long run.

Eve hopped into the shower, and for the first time since the afternoon of the children's Christmas party, allowed her thoughts to focus on Mac and her feelings for him. She'd tried to tell herself that she couldn't be in love with him, that her hormones were out of whack, that she simply felt obligated because he'd helped her through one of the most thrilling and traumatic experiences of her life—the birth of her daughter.

But as she stepped from the shower and began to dry herself, she acknowledged with a heavy heart that what she felt for Mac Kingston couldn't be easily brushed aside. It was stronger and infinitely more profound than anything she'd ever experienced before.

From the first moment she'd seen him and glimpsed that lost and lonely look in the depths of his silver-gray eyes, she'd recognized a kindred spirit. They both knew the meaning of loneliness. They'd both endured an unhappy childhood, and while her circumstances had been the opposite of Mac's, they'd both known the pain of being unloved and unwanted.

She felt sorry for him. Yes. But he'd proved to be resourceful and kind, gentle and caring, someone to count on in a crisis. She'd fallen in love with that caring, tender side, a side he rarely let people see. But once again she'd fallen for the wrong man, and like Larry, Eve was sure, Mac would walk out of her life without a backward glance.

Behind her Hope whimpered, and Eve tiptoed to the crib to check her daughter. The baby slept on, and Eve let out a sigh of relief as she crossed to the closet. Pulling out a pair of black slacks and her favorite red silk blouse she put them on. She left her hair down, brushing it back and tying it with a matching red ribbon. After applying a minimum of makeup, she silently withdrew, leaving the door ajar.

A quick glance at the clock on the stove told her Mac would be arriving any minute.

She'd used a dark-green tablecloth for the table, and among her decorations she'd found a box containing Christmas crackers, left over from last year. Eve began to think the red and green candles she'd put on the table made it look too romantic. But before she could remove them she heard the outer door open. Mac had arrived.

The tap on her door sent her pulse scrambling, and she had to take several steadying breaths before moving to answer it.

"Merry Christmas!" Mac said, flashing his killer smile. "Dinner's right here," he added, holding up a large carrier bag.

"Merry Christmas," Eve replied, thinking he looked far more appealing than the food.

"Oh, and I brought you this." Mac moved to the right and returned holding a two-foot Christmas tree, decorated with several strings of red and green beads and a handful of pretty silver ornaments.

Eve was too stunned to speak.

"I'm afraid I cheated a little," Mac hurried on.

"I phoned around trying to find a tree, with no luck, so I commandeered this one from the restaurant."

Eve smiled, touched that he'd made the effort. "It's perfect, thank you," she told him as she stepped aside to let him in.

Five minutes later Eve stood back to admire the tree she'd set on the round table in the corner.

Mac came to stand beside her. "You sounded disappointed about not having a tree," he said. "Besides, it's Hope's first Christmas, and she should have a tree."

Eve turned to him, her eyes brimming. "I've always believed that there's something special about a Christmas tree. Thank you."

"How is Hope?" he asked.

"She's asleep, at least for the moment. Mmm, dinner smells delicious," she said, the aroma of turkey with sage dressing wafting through the air, reminding her she'd barely had a moment to eat all day.

"My mouth was watering all the way here," Mac said, as he crossed to the kitchen. "The table looks great," he added.

"Thanks," Eve murmured, pleased that he'd noticed. "I'll put your coat in the bedroom and check on Hope while I'm there," Eve said. "I'll be right back."

"No rush."

Mac watched Eve's departing figure, thinking

how lovely she looked wearing red. Reaching for the oven mitts hanging on the side of the stove, he began to remove the hot dishes from the carrier bag.

As he worked he thought about how much he'd been looking forward to spending the evening with Eve. He'd wanted to surprise her with a tree and all the trimmings, and if Eve's reaction was anything to go by, she'd been pleased.

"Everything okay?" he asked when she rejoined him.

"She's still asleep," Eve reported, and Mac could see the worry lines around her eyes.

"Then we should eat right away, in case she wakes up," he said.

"Good idea."

Mac pulled out a kitchen chair for her.

"Oh, just a minute," Eve said. "I almost forgot. I've got a present for you."

Mac frowned as she retrieved a package wrapped in shiny gold paper from a shelf nearby.

"Merry Christmas!" She held the gift out to him.

Mac stared at the brightly wrapped package then at Eve. Her shy smile sent his heart tripping wildly. "You bought me a Christmas present?" His voice sounded hoarse even to his own ears. He couldn't remember the last time someone had given him a present.

"It isn't much," she told him. "I saw it the other

day when Hope and I were out shopping, and I thought of you.''

He met her gaze and watched, fascinated, as her cheeks turned almost the same color as her blouse.

"It's a small thank-you, for all you did when we were at the cabin," she explained in a rush.

"You shouldn't have...I didn't..." He stumbled to a halt, moved immeasurably by the gesture.

"Open it," she said.

Mac cleared his throat, surprised by the emotion churning inside him. With the eagerness and excitement of a child, he tore at the paper to reveal a beautiful leather-bound copy of *The Adventures of Huckleberry Finn*. Unable to speak, he gazed in awe at the beautiful book.

"It's a silly gift. You probably have one. I just thought—" Eve was rambling, and, looking at her, Mac realized she'd interpreted his stunned silence as a negative response, that he didn't like the gift, when in fact the opposite was true.

"No, it's perfect," Mac said. At his words her blue eyes lit up with joy and her sexy mouth curved into a breathtaking smile that sent his heart into overdrive.

"Are you sure? I mean...you must have a copy..." She sounded flustered. Totally charmed, he lost another piece of his heart.

"As a matter of fact I don't." He took a step

toward her. "Thank you, Eve. I shall treasure this," he said, emotion making his voice shaky.

The tiny kitchen suddenly seemed crowded, and the air between them crackled. What was there about this woman that seemed to touch his very soul? Mac wondered, grappling with the urge to haul her into his arms and kiss her. Mesmerized, he watched the tip of her tongue appear and moisten her lips, an action that lit a raging fire deep in his belly. Her very nearness scrambled his senses and shattered his willpower.

Muttering an oath, he closed the gap between them. The moment his mouth touched hers he was lost. The impulse to plunder her softness and demand a response almost overwhelmed him, but he held back, afraid he would hurt her, afraid he would frighten her. Using every ounce of restraint, he tenderly laid siege to her lips with slow, hot, wet kisses that tested his sanity and tortured his soul.

When he felt the tips of her fingers tentatively touch his cheek and her tongue dart into his mouth in an open invitation to dance, his control snapped and he took what she offered.

Mac's mouth, hot and wet on hers aroused sensations and awakened emotions she hadn't known she could feel. His kisses teased and tantalized, inviting her participation rather than demanding a response. She could taste his need, feel his desire, and an answering desire came to life within her, aching to be fulfilled.

Eve had never felt so alive. Larry's kisses had never made her feel like this, so powerful, so desired and yet so cherished at the same time. She realized now that she'd been naive in believing herself in love with Larry. Yes, he'd made her feel special and the fact that he'd wanted her had been exciting, but he'd never aroused these earth-shattering sensations and emotions, nor had he shown her such tenderness.

The sound of the baby's cry penetrated her sensual bubble.

Eve broke free of Mac's arms. "Hope!" she cried and hurried to the bedroom. "It's okay. Mommy's here," she crooned as she lowered the crib side and lifted the crying baby into her arms. Behind her she was aware of Mac standing watching in the doorway.

"She's burning up! There's something wrong." Panicked, she turned to Mac, who came to her side.

He placed his hand on the baby's forehead. "You're right, she is hot. You'd better call your doctor," he suggested.

Tears blurred her vision, but she steadied herself. "Would you call?" she asked. "Her name is Dr. Gray and her number is in the small black book by the phone on the kitchen counter."

"Right," Mac said and strode away.

He found the book and the doctor's number and quickly dialed.

"Dr. Gray's answering service. How may I help you?" a voice asked.

"I'm calling on behalf of Eve Darling, one of Dr. Gray's patients. Eve's baby has awoken with a high temperature. Is it possible for the doctor to come by and take a look at her?"

"I'm sorry sir, Dr. Gray isn't on call tonight. She shares these duties with another doctor, and he's already out on another call," the voice replied. "I can page him."

"We have a sick baby, here," Mac cut in, urgency in his voice.

"In that case, sir, I would suggest you transport the baby to the emergency room yourself."

Eve, with the crying baby in her arms, appeared from the bedroom.

"Thank you. I'll do that." Mac hung up.

"Is Dr. Gray coming?" Eve asked above the baby's cries, anxiety lacing her voice.

Mac came toward her. "Dr. Gray isn't working tonight. They suggested we take Hope to E.R. ourselves."

"But I don't have a car—" Eve began, trying to quell her rising panic.

"I picked up David's truck from the garage yesterday," he told her calmly. "I'll run to the inn and get it. Meet me outside in five minutes."

Before Eve could respond, Mac was headed for the door.

Eve wanted to shout after him to take his coat, but he'd already gone. Easing Hope off her shoulder, she gazed at her daughter's bright-red cheeks and tear-stained face. During her pregnancy she'd read a variety of books on child care, but more concerned about the birth itself she'd skimmed the chapters dealing with illnesses.

She didn't know what she would have done if Mac hadn't been here. He'd taken charge, acting swiftly, and she needed to be ready and waiting when he returned with the truck.

Eve retreated to the bedroom and lowered Hope, still crying, into her crib. Returning to the hallway she pulled on her boots and jacket. Back in the bedroom, she took a blanket from Hope's crib and wrapped it loosely around the baby, then, lifting Hope into her arms once more, hurried to the outer door.

With relief she saw the headlights of David's truck approaching. Mac pulled up at the curb and hopped down from the cab to help her into the passenger seat.

Throughout the short drive to the hospital Hope cried incessantly. Ten minutes later Mac pulled into the emergency area and parked in one of the vacant spots.

Mac came around the truck to help her out. Putting his arm around Eve and the baby, he ushered them across the snow-covered driveway to the emergency room's automatic doors.

Chapter Twelve

Two hours later Eve was pacing outside the isolation room where they'd taken the baby after her initial examination. When the emergency room doctor appeared Eve hurried toward him.

"Hope is a little better," Dr. Samuelson told her. "Her temperature is down slightly, but we still don't know the cause. I'd like to keep her overnight for observation."

"Can't you tell me what's wrong with my baby?" Eve asked, her voice wavering.

Mac appeared at her side, putting his arm around her shoulder. "Eve, I'm sure the doctor is doing all he can."

"We've done a series of tests," the doctor said. "And I should have some answers within the hour."

Eve choked back tears. "I just want to take my baby home."

"Why don't you try to rest for a while," the doctor suggested. "There's a lounge on this floor. The nurse will show you the way. I promise I'll let you know the test results as soon as I have them."

Eve started to protest, but Mac cut in.

"The doctor's right," he said. "You need to rest. You're exhausted. Hope is in good hands."

The doctor nodded then signaled the nurse standing nearby, who led them down the hall and into a small lounge equipped with a sink, a stove, a sofa and a couple of easy chairs.

"Thank you," Mac said as the nurse withdrew.

He turned to Eve. "Would you like a cup of tea?"

"Tea would be nice."

"Sit," he ordered. "I'll make it."

Eve didn't argue. Five minutes later Mac handed her a steaming cup of tea. "Thanks," she said, and took a sip. "I wish there was something I could do. I hate this feeling of helplessness."

Mac sat beside her. "Eve, is there anyone you want me to call? Anyone you'd like to have here with you?"

Eve shook her head. "There's no one. I told you I don't have any relatives, and as for friends, well, it's Christmas night, I wouldn't want to drag anyone away from their family."

Mac said nothing for a moment. "What about

Hope's father? Shouldn't you call him? Doesn't he have a right to know what's happening?''

Stunned, Eve gazed at Mac in astonishment. ''You think I should call Hope's father?''

''You've never spoken about him, and I can only guess that whatever happened between the two of you is still a painful subject. But he is the baby's father,'' Mac said.

Eve closed her eyes for a moment. He was right, talking about Larry was painful, but not for the reasons Mac was implying.

Opening her eyes, she met his gaze. ''Why would I want my daughter to have any contact with a man who's not only a liar and a thief but wanted by the police.''

Shock registered on Mac's face. ''I had no idea...I'm sorry...'' his voice trailed off.

''Didn't David tell you about the scandal?'' Eve continued.

''Scandal?'' Mac repeated. ''No.''

''It involved an old friend of his—''

''Wait,'' Mac interrupted, his expression clearing. ''David did say something about an acquaintance from high school showing up in town. Are you saying this guy stole from David?''

''Not from David. But from a dozen or so gullible fools.'' She set the cup down on the table in front of her. ''But I was the biggest fool of all,'' she went on in a self-deprecating tone. ''That he tricked me out of my life savings was bad enough, but he also told me he loved me and wanted to marry me.

"Silly me, I believed him. But everything he told me was a lie. And once he had everyone's money, he hightailed it out of town. The police are still looking for him, and there are other charges, too. Oh, and did I mention he already has a wife?"

Mac heard the anger and pain in Eve's words and could have kicked himself for bringing up the subject. He'd put both feet right in it.

David had told him about the incident, saying he'd felt both responsible and guilty that he'd been the one who'd introduced the con man to his friends. But David hadn't mentioned Eve.

Mac realized that Eve had not only lost her savings, but she'd been seduced and betrayed by the man she'd loved. Anger the like of which he'd never known burned within him. Despite what she'd gone through, she'd accepted her predicament, faced it head-on, making the decision to keep her baby. Hope was fortunate indeed to be loved so unconditionally by her mother. His admiration for Eve rose another notch.

"Eve, I'm sorry. I had no idea." Mac wished he could erase the pain and heartache she'd suffered. Now he understood why David had left her his legacy, understood and approved.

"All that matters right now is my baby," Eve said, her voice breaking.

Mac put his arm around her again. "Hope's going to be fine," he said, silently praying he was right.

"She has to be…she means everything to me."

"Me, too," Mac mumbled under his breath, but his words were drowned out by the sound of the door behind them opening.

They turned in unison to see Dr. Samuelson in the doorway. Eve shot to her feet and hurried forward.

"Your daughter's fine," he said with a smile. "Her temperature is back to normal, and I'm happy to report that all the test results have come back negative."

Relief slammed into Eve. "Thank you, Doctor," she said in a choked voice, hastily wiping away the stray tears sliding down her cheek. "Can I see her? Can I take her home?"

"Yes, you can see her," he responded. "But I'd still like her to stay till morning."

Eve's anxiety returned. "But, I thought…"

"It's just a precaution," he assured her. "The nurses will monitor her temperature for the remainder of the night and keep me posted."

"I see," Eve said. "Can I stay with her?"

"Of course," he replied. "And to ease your mind a little, let me say that it's not uncommon for babies or young children to be brought in with a high temperature, then sent home a few hours later without us ever knowing the cause of it. It's worrisome, I know, but trust me, babies are very resilient, and Hope is no exception.''

Eve managed a smile.

''I'll stop by in the morning before I go off duty,'' the doctor continued. ''In the meantime you and your husband can see your daughter.''

Blinking back tears, Eve nodded.

''Thank you for all you've done,'' Mac said as the doctor withdrew.

Eve turned to Mac. ''I'm sorry about the misunderstanding.''

''Don't be,'' he said. ''Let's go and see Hope.''

Together they made their way down the corridor. When they entered the room, Hope was crying, but Eve could see the baby's color had returned to normal. By the familiar, fussy sounds, she knew that Hope was hungry.

With a sharp sense of relief, Eve took the baby from the nurse. ''She's hungry,'' she said, darting a smile at Mac as she kissed Hope's forehead.

Mac reached out to gently caress the baby's cheek, and Eve could have sworn she saw a glimmer of moisture in his gray eyes. ''I'll be outside if you need me,'' he said, his voice barely above a whisper.

''Did Dr. Samuelson tell you he wants to monitor the baby for the rest of the night?'' the nurse asked once Mac had left the room.

''Yes,'' Eve replied. ''And he said I could stay.''

''I'll get a roll-away cot sent up,'' the nurse said.

Eve unbuttoned her blouse and carried the baby to the nearby chair. The baby nursed hungrily and as Eve gazed down at the tiny bundle in her arms, her heart expanded with love and gratitude.

She'd just finished feeding the baby when the nurse wheeled in a cot, blankets and a pillow. Reluctant to put Hope down, Eve sat holding her long after Hope had fallen asleep. Mac didn't reappear, and Eve guessed he must have gone back to the condo.

Fearful she might doze off with the baby still in her arms, she rose and placed Hope in the safety of the crib. With a tired sigh she climbed onto the cot nearby and, exhausted from the ordeal, immediately drifted off to sleep.

Eve didn't hear the door open a few minutes later, nor was she aware of Mac crossing to the crib. He stood for a long time staring down at the sleeping child before moving to the cot where Eve lay. Taking the folded blanket from the foot of the bed, he spread it over Eve before returning to his post outside the door.

It was foolish to stay, but even if he returned to the condo he knew he wouldn't sleep. The hospital staff assumed he was Eve's husband and Hope's father and, to his surprise, he found the idea appealing.

Mac snorted softly. Fool! After hearing Eve's story, he doubted she'd be interested in any man.

And besides, Hope needed a father, and his parenting skills were nonexistent.

But Eve *had* complimented him on how confidently he handled Hope during the birth and afterward. That had to count for something. He doubted that confidence, even with his stint as Santa Claus, qualified him for fatherhood.

He had learned something interesting while playing Santa. Kids liked to be listened to, and they seemed to know if you were talking down to them. They also responded well to praise. Joe and Maggie Kingston had constantly told him how pleased they were with him, how proud they were of his improving grades and changed behavior.

Maybe parenting wasn't as difficult as he thought. Every child blossomed under the care and attention of two loving parents. He certainly had, during the five years he'd spent with the Kingstons.

Mac closed his eyes, imagining himself at Eve's side, as her husband and lover...and as Hope's father.

It was past six o'clock when Hope's familiar morning cooing noises awakened Eve. She lay on her back for a few moments, savoring the sweet sounds.

Later, after feeding the baby, as Eve wrapped Hope in her blanket in readiness for going home, there was a knock on the door. She turned to see

Mac, dressed in the same clothes he'd worn the night before. Her heart skipped a beat at the sight of his rumpled clothes and unshaven jaw.

"Didn't you go home?" she asked.

"It hardly seemed worth it," Mac replied easily. "How is Hope this morning?"

"She's as right as rain, thank heavens," Eve replied, touched by the knowledge that he'd spent the night at the hospital.

"That's good to hear," Mac said.

Another tap sounded on the door, and this time Dr. Samuelson appeared.

"Good morning!" the doctor greeted them. "How is my young patient this morning?"

"She's fine," Eve told him. "Her temperature has been normal all night. Did the nurses tell you?"

"Yes," he acknowledged. "I've already signed the release forms. You can take her home anytime."

A half hour later Mac brought the truck to a halt outside the condo.

"You must be exhausted," Eve said. "I don't know how to thank you for all you've done," she told him as he helped her out of the truck.

"No problem, I'm glad I could be of help. Too bad about Christmas dinner, though," he added on a lighter note. "I was looking forward to turkey with all the trimmings."

"Oh, dear, I forgot all about the dinner," Eve said as Mac unlocked the front door.

"If Chef asks, we'll say it was delicious," he said

once they were inside. "Do you need a hand cleaning up?" he offered.

"Thanks, but I'll manage. Besides, you've done
more than enough already."

"In that case I think I'll take a quick shower and
head up to the inn."

"You're going in to work?" she asked, surprised.

Mac shrugged his shoulders. "I have some calls
I need to follow up on."

"Oh, right." Eve managed to smile. He was talking, of course, about his quest to find a buyer for
his portion of the inheritance.

"I'll stop by later and pick up the book you gave
me," Mac said before turning toward the stairs.

Eve let herself in and carried Hope through to the
bedroom. As she lowered the sleeping baby into the
crib she noticed Mac's coat on the bed. Thinking he
might need it, she picked it up and retraced her steps
to the outer hallway.

She crossed to the stairs and started to climb.
From above she could hear the sound of running
water telling her he was already in the shower. Un-
bidden came an image of Mac naked, with water
cascading onto his dark head, over his broad shoulders and down his muscled body.

A shiver of longing chased through her.

A phone rang in David's living room. Fearful
Mac might suddenly appear to answer it she raced
to the top of the stairs and dropped the coat over the
newel post. By the time she started back down, Da-

vid's answering machine had kicked in and Eve heard a stranger's voice.

"Mac, it's me, Ethan," the caller said. "I tried calling you at the inn but you weren't there, so they gave me this number. I've been thinking about your call the other day. I'm interested, very interested.

"I wanted to give you a heads-up. I'm going to pay you a visit to check things out in person. I should be there sometime this afternoon. See you then."

Eve stood frozen, unable to move. While she'd known it was only a matter of time before Mac found a buyer, she hadn't expected it to be quite so soon.

All at once she realized she couldn't hear the water running. Mac was out of the shower. Jolted into action, she scurried down the stairs and into her room. Heart pounding, she closed the door and leaned against it, trying to catch her breath.

A few moments later she headed for the kitchen and began to clear away the food and the dishes. As she worked, her thoughts drifted over the hours spent at the hospital.

Mac had been her strength and her support, helping her stay calm while the doctors checked Hope. She didn't know how she would have made it through the ordeal if he hadn't been there. If she hadn't already been in love with him, she'd have fallen for him then. But falling for Mac Kingston was an even bigger mistake than falling for Larry Dawson.

On reflection what she felt for Larry hadn't been love, at all. She'd been flattered by his attention and seduced by his charm, but it had been her own deep longing to be loved, to be wanted, that had blinded her to the fact that Larry had been using her. When she'd learned about his betrayal, she hadn't been totally surprised, not really.

Mac Kingston, on the other hand, had used neither flattery nor charm to win her heart. His actions had spoken far louder than any words. During their time at the cabin he'd revealed himself to be a resourceful and dependable man in a crisis, a man who would never turn his back on someone in need. And even though he tried to give the impression he was both cold and unfeeling, behind the facade lurked a tender and caring man, a man who would make Hope a wonderful father.

Mac replaced the receiver and leaned back in the leather rocking chair that had been his brother's. Mac's head ached, due no doubt to the sleepless night he'd endured and to the fact that from the moment he'd walked through the front door of the inn he'd been dealing with a number of things, all urgent, all requiring his personal attention. He stretched and gazed up at the tiled ceiling. His thoughts turning, as they did more and more these days, to Eve and the baby.

What a night, he thought. He'd felt so damned helpless watching Eve struggle not to break down and weep, while Hope cried incessantly. Witnessing the emotional toll the night had taken on Eve and the baby, the two people he'd grown to care about more than he was willing to admit, had torn at his heart and twisted his insides into knots. He knew he shouldn't feel such deep-rooted responsibility toward Hope but, in a secret place in his heart, he regarded her as his own daughter. No doubt the fact that he'd helped bring Hope into the world, catching her in his bare hands as she slid from her mother's womb, was the reason his feelings were so strong.

Then there was Eve, the woman who'd shown him the true meaning of courage, who with her heart-stopping smile and steely determination had played a big part in melting the frozen wasteland that had surrounded his heart. With a muttered oath Mac slammed his hands on the desk and leaped to his feet. Was he in love with her? Was that why he couldn't settle, couldn't stop thinking about her, why he longed to be back at the condo with them?

What other explanation could there be for the emotions that erupted like a volcano whenever he thought of her and whenever she was near?

Mac began to pace. He tried to tell himself he was mistaken. What did he know about love? Hadn't he made it his life's work to steer clear of involvements and romantic entanglements?

Yes, they'd shared a few electrifying kisses, and they'd been through a lot together, but being responsible for Eve's happiness, taking on the job of parenting a child— The idea, quite frankly, scared him to death.

Mac ran his hand through his hair and massaged the back of his neck. He tried to tell himself Eve and Hope's welfare weren't any of his concern, that once he found a buyer for the properties, he would get on the first plane back to Switzerland.

Who was he trying to fool? He no more wanted to return to his solitary life in Switzerland than he wanted to fly to the moon. What he wanted was to stay in Cypress Crossing, to make a life here with Eve and Hope.

What did he have to lose? Being around Eve and Hope was reason enough to stay, and by staying he could fulfill his brother's dream. And maybe, just maybe, maybe make his own dreams come true.

A loud knock, followed by the sound of a familiar voice startled Mac. He spun around to see Ethan Saunders, the businessman and property developer he'd contacted in the hope that Ethan would be interested in buying him out. Now, however, he didn't want to sell.

"Ethan! This is a surprise. What brings you here?" Mac said as he rose and came around the desk.

"Didn't you get my message?" Ethan asked as they shook hands. "I called the inn this morning, but you weren't around. They gave me another number to try, and I left a message on the machine telling you I'd be dropping by."

"I guess I missed it," Mac said. "It's good to see you. Take your coat off. Have a seat. I assume this unexpected visit has something to do with those properties I told you about.''

''That's right,'' Ethan replied. ''And as I happened to be spending Christmas in Vancouver, I thought I'd fly up here and take a look around.''

''I'm sorry to say you've made the trip for nothing,'' Mac said.

''You mean you've got another buyer?'' Ethan asked.

''No, I've changed my mind. I'm not going to sell, after all.''

Ethan tossed his coat over a nearby chair. ''That's too bad. The golf course project you mentioned sounded appealing. I've come all this way—the least you could do is let me take a look at the plans.''

Mac smiled. ''Sure. They're right here. Pull up a chair.''

Eve had been listening for Mac's return for some time. She had to assume the caller who'd left the message had arrived. Even now he and Mac might be signing the papers.

She checked her runaway thoughts. Even if Mac had found a buyer, a considerable amount of paperwork would have to be done before any change could take place. Besides it was Boxing Day, and she doubted Debra's office was open.

Why couldn't Mac have been excited about David's plans for the golf course and clubhouse? Then he'd have been staying on to see that David's dream came true. And maybe, just maybe, he would have come to realize how much she and Hope needed him.

Eve silently chided herself. Fool! Why should she think he'd be interested in her or in taking on another man's child? She had a great deal to be thankful for. She had a healthy, happy baby. And, thanks to David, her financial worries were over. But Eve couldn't help wishing for that romantic happy ending, like the ones in the romance novels she loved to read.

The sound of the outer door caught her attention. With her heart drumming noisily against her breast, she held her breath and waited for Mac to knock. When she heard the sound of deep male voices followed by heavy footsteps on the stairs, she knew Mac wasn't alone. Exhaling, she tried to tell herself that it didn't matter. It was time she forgot about Mac Kingston and got on with the rest of her life.

Chapter Thirteen

It was eight o'clock before Eve managed to get Hope settled in her crib. Returning to the living room, she picked up her plate and cup, remnants from the sandwich and tea that had been her evening meal, and carried them to the kitchen.

When the phone on the counter rang, she grabbed it before it could ring a second time.

"Eve, it's Mac." The low, familiar voice sent her pulse scrambling.

"Hi," she replied.

"I'm not calling too late, am I?" he asked. "You're not in the middle of feeding Hope?"

"No. She's asleep," she told him.

"How has she been today?"

"Fine," she said, keeping her answers brief.

"Ah, listen, would it be all right if we popped down for a few minutes?" he said. "There's someone here I'd like you to meet. And I want to pick up my book."

Eve hesitated, not sure she was ready to see Mac or the man with him, no doubt the one who'd left a message on David's answering machine.

"Okay," she replied at last.

"Thanks. We'll be right down."

Eve scanned the living room, her gaze lingering for a moment on the Christmas tree Mac had brought with him on Christmas day. She heard footsteps on the stairs and, moving to the door, opened it before Mac could knock.

"Hi." Mac greeted her. "I'd like to introduce you to a friend of mine, Ethan Saunders. Ethan, this is Eve Darling."

Ethan smiled and extended his hand. "It's a pleasure to meet you, Eve. Mac has told me a lot about you."

"Really?" Eve shook the hand he offered. "It's nice to meet you," she added, wondering just what Mac had told him.

"Won't you sit down?" she invited once they'd reached the living room. "Can I get you anything?"

"Not for me, thank you," Ethan replied as he lowered his tall frame into the easy chair.

Eve turned to Mac.

"Nothing, thanks." He dropped onto the sofa.

"Ethan and I have spent the last few hours poring over David's plans," Mac said, getting right to the point. "He's impressed and very keen to be a part of it all."

"You like the plans?" Eve asked, her tone strangely detached.

"I do," Ethan enthused. "The project should take a year and a half to complete, but when it's done it'll draw an influx of people to the area, not to mention generating a substantial revenue."

"Ethan thinks we should start construction early in the spring," Mac said.

"And if everything goes according to plan," Ethan continued, "the facility should be ready to open a year next summer."

"Sounds like the two of you have worked it all out," Eve commented dryly.

Mac frowned. "I thought you'd be pleased. I thought making David's dream a reality was what you wanted," he said, obviously puzzled by her attitude.

"I am pleased," she said, sounding the exact opposite. "I just hoped—"

What was the point in telling Mac what she'd hoped for? It appeared he'd made the decision to sell, and telling him she'd hoped he'd stay in Cypress Crossing, oversee the project and play a part not only in his brother's dream but also in hers and her daughter's would be an exercise in futility.

Ethan rose. "I should get back to the inn," he
said. "I have some calls to make. Luckily, Mac
managed to get me a room. I'm heading back to
Vancouver tomorrow afternoon, but Mac's promised
to take me for a drive out to the site in the morning."

Eve darted a glance at Mac. "I hope you're planning on checking the weather report before you set
out."

Mac smiled. "Definitely."

"Eve, it's been my pleasure," Ethan said. "Mac
drives a hard bargain. After the lawyers finish
thrashing out the contract, we should get together
and celebrate. We're going to make a great team."
He flashed a grin and headed for the door.

Eve turned to Mac. "How long do you think it
will take the lawyers to…thrash things out?" Eve
asked.

"Ethan plans to set things in motion in the next
day or two," Mac said. "And we could probably
set up a meeting with Deb, say…early in the New
Year."

"So it's a done deal," Eve said, trying to ignore
the pain squeezing her heart. The completion of the
deal would signal Mac's departure from Cypress
Crossing.

"You could say that," Mac replied.

"And you'll be leaving."

Mac hesitated. "I wanted to talk to you about that."

"What's there to talk about?" Eve asked, wishing he would go. The longer he stayed the harder it would be to say goodbye.

"Hold on. Let me see Ethan on his way." Mac didn't wait for an answer but hurried after his friend.

Eve began to pace the small living room.

When Mac reappeared, a shiver chased down her spine that had nothing to do with the cold air he brought with him and everything to do with the fact that she was already beginning to miss him.

"Are you cold?" Mac asked, concern on his face as he approached.

"I'm fine," Eve replied, stepping back, determined to keep him at arm's length. "You were saying?"

"First, tell me if I'm wrong, but I got the distinct impression you have some reservations about Ethan."

"Not at all. I'm just surprised you were able to find someone willing to buy you out so quickly," she said.

Mac gave her a strange look. "What do you mean buy me out?"

Eve frowned. "You've made it plain from the start that you wanted to sell your portion of David's legacy and go back to Switzerland."

"That's true," Mac acknowledged.

"And if I'm not mistaken, Ethan is the buyer you've been looking for."

"Ethan and I have made a deal, but it isn't what you think," Mac said.

Eve held his gaze for a long moment. "I don't understand."

"Ethan came here because he was interested in buying me out, only I changed my mind," Mac said.

At his words Eve's heart rammed against her breastbone in reaction. She swallowed convulsively.

"Changed your mind? About what?" she asked.

"About selling and about leaving," Mac told her, and because he'd wanted to see her reaction, he caught the flicker of joy that lit up her lovely blue eyes.

"You're not leaving?" Eve repeated.

"I'm not leaving. I told Ethan I'd changed my mind, but having made a special trip here he insisted on seeing the plans. He became very excited, then he asked if he could buy into the project."

"And you agreed."

"If you remember, I did mention to you that David's project would need financial backing. That's where Ethan comes in—he wants to be the backer. He has the kind of contacts and expertise, not to mention money, that we'll need in order to pull off a project of this size."

"What made you change your mind?" she asked.

"Ever since you got here you've given me the impression that you couldn't wait to leave."

Mac took a step closer. He wasn't sure he could find the right words to tell her that he was tired of running, tired of being alone, that she and Hope were the reasons he'd changed his mind.

"That was true the day I arrived," Mac acknowledged. "But it isn't true any longer."

"I don't understand," Eve said with a frown.

"Ever since I was a kid moving from one foster home to another, I made a vow that I'd never let myself get too close to anyone, never get emotionally involved. Because every time I let myself care, or I started to feel like I belonged, I'd do something stupid and get hauled out of the foster home and placed in another.

"When I was sent to spend Christmas with the Kingston family I didn't want to like them, didn't want to care about them. I tested their patience, believe me, but Maggie and Joe and David refused to give up on me, and slowly they wore me down and won me over.

"For the next five years I learned what is was like to be part of a family, to be loved. But all that ended the day Maggie and Joe died.

"I was devastated. David was, too, of course," he went on. "But I was also very angry. I refused to let him comfort me. I rejected his invitation to stay with him, and I ran."

"And you've been running ever since," Eve said, almost to herself.

Mac raked a hand through his hair and met her gaze. "Would you believe me if I told you that right now I'm scared out of my mind, shaking like a leaf inside, and my instincts are telling me to run?"

Startled, Eve wasn't sure if she understood. "Are you saying you're afraid of me?"

At her words Eve saw the vulnerability in the depths of his gray eyes, and her heart went out to him.

"In a way I suppose I am," Mac confessed.

"But—" Eve began, but Mac held up his hand to silence her.

"Let me rephrase that," Mac said. "It's not you I'm scared of, Eve, it's the feelings I have for you. I've never felt like this about anyone," he confessed.

Her heart glowing, her head reeling, Eve could scarcely believe Mac had just admitted he had feelings for her—deep feelings.

"What would you say if I told you I have feelings for you, too?" Eve replied, and caught the glimmer of hope that flashed in his eyes.

"I'd say I'm more scared than ever," he replied. "And after all you've been through already, I wouldn't blame you if you wanted to go it alone.

"Hope needs a father," he went on, "someone to love her and guide her. Though, in all honesty I'm not qualified for the job. I know nothing about parenting, about raising a child.''

''And you think I do?'' Eve replied. ''I'm scared to death every day that I'll make a mistake. Raising a child is a huge responsibility and one I'm not sure I'm qualified for, either.''

''But you're her mother,'' Mac responded in a startled tone.

She laughed softly. ''That's true, but it doesn't mean I know what I'm doing. I'm bound to make mistakes, but isn't that how we learn and grow?

''We can learn together, Mac. All we have to do is love her and try to do what's best for her. I'm willing to give it a try if you are.''

''What if I screw up?'' Mac asked still not convinced. ''What if...''

Eve brought her finger to his lips. ''What if I screw up?'' she countered, and waited with bated breath for his answer. ''There are no guarantees,'' she told him.

''But...''

''There are all kinds of books on parenting, and they'll help, I'm sure. But I believe loving Hope is the most important thing you can do for her. You do love her, don't you?''

''Like she was my own,'' Mac said, his voice vibrating with emotion.

Tears stung her eyes at his words. ''She is yours, Mac, in every way that's important,'' Eve said in a hoarse whisper. "You were there for her during the storm when she was born and again last night when we took her to the hospital. She needs you. And I know you'll be a wonderful father."

"What about you, Eve? Do you need me?" he asked, his voice wavering. She met his gaze, seeing that look of fear and vulnerability again.

"Yes," she breathed, unable to believe this was happening. "I love you, Mac. I didn't really know what love was until you came into my life."

Mac felt his heart explode at her words and the sincerity behind them. Until this woman came into his life, no one had ever touched him so profoundly. He wasn't sure he deserved her, or her love, or this miracle that was happening.

"And I love you, Eve Darling," he said, his words as clear and true as the emotions bursting from his heart. "I never thought I'd say that to anyone, but with you, it's easy."

A tiny sob escaped Eve's lips, and Mac pulled her against him in a fierce embrace.

"Let's get married, now, tonight," he said.

Eve eased away, laughter bubbling to the surface. "Tonight?" she repeated.

"Okay, tomorrow, then. Or, I know, what about New Year's Eve?"

"Are you sure?" Eve asked.

"I've never been more sure of anything in my

life,'' he answered. ''That way we can start the New Year together as a family. What do you say?''

''Yes!'' She practically shouted the word, and Mac laughed as he lifted her off her feet and spun her around.

''Do you think David would approve?'' he asked, slowing to a halt.

Hot tears began to trickle down her face. ''I think he's smiling down on us right now,'' she said thickly.

''It's true, then,'' Mac said.

''What's true?'' Eve asked.

''Miracles do happen at Christmas,'' he answered, then his mouth covered hers.

Eve returned Mac's kiss with all the love in her heart, knowing this was one Christmas she would always remember.

*   *   *   *   *

If you enjoyed what you just read,
then we've got an offer you can't resist!

Take 2 bestselling love stories FREE!

Plus get a FREE surprise gift!

Clip this page and mail it to Silhouette Reader Service™

IN U.S.A.	IN CANADA
3010 Walden Ave.	P.O. Box 609
P.O. Box 1867	Fort Erie, Ontario
Buffalo, N.Y. 14240-1867	L2A 5X3

YES! Please send me 2 free Silhouette Romance® novels and my free surprise gift. After receiving them, if I don't wish to receive anymore, I can return the shipping statement marked cancel. If I don't cancel, I will receive 6 brand-new novels every month, before they're available in stores! In the U.S.A., bill me at the bargain price of $3.34 plus 25¢ shipping and handling per book and applicable sales tax, if any*. In Canada, bill me at the bargain price of $3.80 plus 25¢ shipping and handling per book and applicable taxes**. That's the complete price and a savings of at least 10% off the cover prices—what a great deal! I understand that accepting the 2 free books and gift places me under no obligation ever to buy any books. I can always return a shipment and cancel at any time. Even if I never buy another book from Silhouette, the 2 free books and gift are mine to keep forever.

215 SDN DNUM
315 SDN DNUN

Name	(PLEASE PRINT)	
Address	Apt.#	
City	State/Prov.	Zip/Postal Code

* Terms and prices subject to change without notice. Sales tax applicable in N.Y.
** Canadian residents will be charged applicable provincial taxes and GST.
  All orders subject to approval. Offer limited to one per household and not valid to
  current Silhouette Romance® subscribers.
® are registered trademarks of Harlequin Books S.A., used under license.

SROM02   ©1998 Harlequin Enterprises Limited

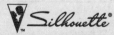

SILHOUETTE Romance

COMING NEXT MONTH

#1630 THE WOLF'S SURRENDER—Sandra Steffen
The Coltons

Kelly Madison had been the bane of the Honorable Grey Colton's existence. Now the feisty defense attorney was back in town, in his courtroom…and ready to give birth! Grey helped deliver her baby—and, to his surprise, softened toward the single mom. But would his ambitions drive him up the legal ladder—or into Kelly's arms?

#1631 LIONHEARTED—Diana Palmer
Long, Tall Texans

Inexperienced debutante Janie Brewster had been chasing successful rancher Leo Hart for years—but he only saw her as a child. At a friend's suggestion, she set out to prove herself a bona fide cowgirl. But would her rough-and-tumble image be enough to win over a sexy, stubborn Hart?

#1632 GUESS WHO'S COMING FOR CHRISTMAS?—Cara Colter

Beth Cavell promised her orphaned nephew snow for Christmas—then handsome Scrooge Riley Keenan appeared and threatened all her plans. When an unexpected storm forced them to spend the holiday together, Beth wondered if Riley could grant Jamie's other Christmas wish—a new daddy!

#1633 THE MARQUIS AND THE MOTHER-TO-BE—Valerie Parv
The Carramer Legacy

The Marquis of Merrisand might be royalty, but that didn't mean that he could claim Carissa Day's lodge as his own! Except that it *was* his, and Carissa was the victim of a con man. A true gentleman, would Eduard de Marigny open his home—and his heart—to the pregnant temptress?

#1634 THE BILLIONAIRE BORROWS A BRIDE—Myrna Mackenzie
The Wedding Auction

Wanting no part of romance, Spencer Fairfield hired Kate Ryerson to pose as his fiancée—after all, Kate supposedly had a fiancé of her own so there would be no expectations. But his ruse wasn't working the way he'd planned, and soon Spencer discovered the only man Kate did have in her life—was himself!

#1635 THE DOCTOR'S PREGNANT PROPOSAL—Donna Clayton
The Thunder Clan

Devastatingly handsome Grey Thunder wasn't interested in a real marriage—but he *was* interested in a pretend one! Marrying the emotionally scarred doctor was the perfect solution to pregnant Lori Young's problems. But could their tentative yet passionate bond help them face the pain of their pasts?

SRCNM1102